Stéphanie Genlis

Tales of the Castle

Or, stories of instruction and delight. Being Les veillées du château. Vol. 4

Stéphanie Genlis

Tales of the Castle

Or, stories of instruction and delight. Being Les veillées du château. Vol. 4

ISBN/EAN: 9783337087838

Printed in Europe, USA, Canada, Australia, Japan

Cover: Foto ©Andreas Hilbeck / pixelio.de

More available books at **www.hansebooks.com**

TALES OF THE CASTLE:

OR,

STORIES

OF

INSTRUCTION AND DELIGHT.

BEING

LES VEILLEES DU CHATEAU,

WRITTEN IN FRENCH

By MADAME LA COMTESSE DE GENLIS,

AUTHOR OF THE THEATRE OF EDUCATION,
ADELA AND THEODORE, &c.

TRANSLATED INTO ENGLISH

By THOMAS HOLCROFT.

Come raccende il gusto il mutar' esca,
Così mi par, che la mia Istoria, quanto
Or quà, or là più variata sia,
Meno a chi l'odirà nojosa sia.   ARIOSTO.

As at the board, with plenteous Viands grac'd,
Cate after Cate excites the sickening taste,
So, while my Muse pursues her varied strains,
The following Tale the ravish'd ear detains.   HOOLE.

The SECOND EDITION.

VOL. IV.

LONDON:
PRINTED FOR G. G. J. and J. ROBINSON,
Nº. 25, PATER-NOSTER-ROW.

MDCCLXXXV.

STORIES

OF

INSTRUCTION AND DELIGHT.

———————

THE Baronnefs ceafed to fpeak; but as it was not late, the company did not immediately break up. I am highly delighted, faid M. de la Paliniére, with the defcription of Angel Sound, the good old woman of ninety-five, and the re-paft at which the Baron was prefent; it recalls to my mind one of the moft charming feafts I ever beheld.

O pray defcribe it.

Willingly——It was in Ruffia. During the month of July, I was travelling through Livonia (*a*), with a Ruffian friend, who was defirous of ftopping at a Relation's country-feat. I was ftruck with the afpect of this habitation, which rather refembled a fmall town than a houfe. It was compofed of a large building, furrounded by twelve fmaller compartments, each connected with the other by covered galleries.

It was nine o'clock in the morning when we arrived at this vaft manfion. We found all the domeftics in a great hurry. My friend afked for Novorgêve (that was the name of their Mafter) and was anfwered, that one of his grand-daughters was juft brought to-bed. Since that is the cafe, faid my friend, we will go and take a walk in the wood; and accordingly we went.

As we walked, I was inquifitive, and my friend replied, Novorgêve is a venerable old man of feventy-five, and poffeffes a large fortune, entirely of his own acquiring. On this fpot was he born, but it was in a cottage. His father was a Farmer, and only owned the fmall lands that lie round here, and the copfe in which we now are. At fourteen, young Novorgêve went to Riga, under the care of a Merchant, who was related to his father. His induftry and underftanding were fo evident, that his relation the Merchant conceived

(*a*) Livonia is one of the fineft provinces in all Ruffia; the land is fo fertile, that it is called the Granary of the North. Riga, a large and rich town, is its capital.

the

the greatest hopes of him; and giving him letters
of recommendation, sent him to Peterburg, certain, that in order to succeed, he wanted only to
be known.

In a country, where, without the advantages of
birth, men may aspire to honourable employments
and dignities, the young Novorgêve could not fail
to make his fortune; he soon found protectors,
and went at first into the army, whence, after
having proved his conduct was equal to his courage, he was recalled, and fixed at Court. About
this time he had the misfortune to lose his father.
He had two Sisters left, who constantly refused
every offer of fraternal assistance. These Sisters,
who were models of the most affecting friendship,
and of moderation still more uncommon, would
never marry, that they might never be asunder:
they were perfectly satisfied with the state in which
their destiny had placed them.

Seduced by ambition, Novorgêve sought and
obtained a wife among the Great. She conducted
herself with decency; but she made him unhappy
by her haughtiness and pride. She died, and left
him six children; three boys and three girls, the
eldest of whom was eight years old. Novorgêve
then resigned all his employments, and asked permission to retire. Hitherto he had only lived in splen-
and perturbation; at last he wished for peace,

quitted the Court, and rejoined his fifters, never to leave them more.

As foon as he came here he built this vaft manfion, but he erazed not the humble dwelling of his father, which ftands at the other end of this wood; to him it is a kind of facred temple, and is vifited by him every day. His employment is the education of his children, to which his Sifters like-wife moft affiduoufly contribute. Nor did he ne-glect to renew his acquaintance with the Farmers, who had been the old friends of his father, as foon as he returned to this his native country; for after he had carefully examined the interior of their families, he chofe, from among them, wives and hufbands for his children.

In confequence of this project, he himfelf un-dertook to direct the education of the children he intended for his future fons and daughters-in-law. This education was not what the world in general underftands by a good one; he was only defirous that they fhould learn to read, write, and caft ac-compts; but he was particularly affiduous that their manners fhould be gentle, their morals pure, their piety fincere, and their time well employed. His virtuous defigns fucceeded according to his wifhes; he has married his children as he projected, and there is no father whofe happinefs can equal his. All living under the fame roof, his numerous fa-mily increafes every year; fo that he has been obliged

obliged, fucceffively, to build the twelve additional compartments which furround his manfion. Here he lives like a Patriarch, with his two refpectable Sifters, and a multitude of children and grand-children, all clothed like himfelf and his fore-fathers; that is to fay, like countrymen and wo-men; but each enjoying every convenience of life, and tafting a happinefs which is fo little fought, only becaufe it is fo little known.

As my friend finifhed his recital, I remarked, there was upon each tree an Infcription, bear-ing a Date and a Name; and I afked him what was the meaning of this fingularity?

In order to underftand it, faid he, it is neceffary to inform you of an ancient cuftom in this coun-try, the origin of which is unknown to me. At the birth of each child, the father of the family plants a tree, on which he infcribes the name of the infant, and the year of it's birth (a). Thus each proprietor of land, if but a little extended, pof-feffes one of thefe facred woods, where the axe never wounds the tree in its vigour; but as foon as it begins to decay, it is then cut down, which is not done without great ceremony.

The family and the neighbours are affembled, the tree is felled in their prefence, and its Infcrip-

(a) It is very true, that this cuftom exifts in Ruffia; but I am not certain it is in the province of Livonia.

tion;

tion entered in a Regifter, with a formal memo-
randum of the year in which it was cut down.
The friends and relations fign the writing as having been witneffes of the procedure; and thefe
Regifters preferve the names and memories of our
anceftors with the greater certitude, becaufe there
is an entry made in another Regifter of the birth of
the infant, and a defcription of the fpecies of tree
that has been planted in the family wood, on the
day of its birth.

While my friend was fpeaking, we heard at a
diftance the found of ruftic mufic. Let us meet
them, faid he, they are going to plant the tree of
the child who was born this morning, and we
fhall fee the venerable Novorgêve attended by a
numerous train. We cannot fpeak to him juft at
this inftant; but after the ceremony he will join us,
and invite us to dinner.

We quickened our pace, and, guided by the
mufic, arrived in a copfe or kind of nurfery, full
of young trees; where we found affembled fome
two hundred people, including about a fcore of
young children. They were all clothed according
to the cuftom of the Livonian Peafants: the drefs of
the men had nothing in it remarkable, but I
thought that of the women agreeable and pictur-
efque; they had folds of muflin about their heads,
which hid only a part of their hair, but which
flowed down and covered all their fhoulders: they

all

all had brown jackets, fringed ftuff girdles, and petticoats richly embroidered.

As I advanced, I difcovered in the midft of this crowd, an old man, of a mild, yet majeftic prefence, clothed like the other Peafants, but whofe fimple and coarfe habit formed a very fingular contraft to the brilliant order he wore. It was a large white Ribband, pendent to which was a magnificent Crofs, enriched with diamonds (a). That is Novorgêve, faid my Guide, as you will eafily imagine, from the fingularity of his appearance. The badge of diftinction he wears, is doubtlefs dear to his heart; it is gradtude, and not pride, which makes him bear with joy this honourable badge of his Sovereign's benevolence.

Be kind enough to tell me, faid I, who that young man is that ftands on his right hand?

One of his grandfons, replied my friend, and the father of the child newly born. Thofe two venerable Women on his left are his aged Sifters; and all the reft that ftand immediately next to him are his defcendants.

How many do you fuppofe them to be?

Nearly fifty people, reckoning his fons and daughters-in-law, and they all live in the manfion-houfe you have feen. The reft of the af-

(a) The Order of St. Andrew, inftituted by the Czar Peter I.

B 4

fembly

fembly is compofed of the relations, neighbours, and friends of the family. But hufh! the ceremony is going to begin.

I drew as near to the old man as poffible, faw him take a fpade, and, with an arm ftill vigorous, open the earth and plant the tree. When this was done, he, according to cuftom, pronounced feveral benedictions over it: he prayed that the tree might flourifh, as long as the *Fir, Peter Novorgéve* (the oldeft tree in the wood,) and that the infant, whofe name it bore, might fit beneath its fhade, with the children of his grand-children.

When he had ended, the Regifter was brought, in which the principal perfons of the Affembly wrote their names. After which Novorgéve received the young infant in his arms, and the proceffion again began to the found of mufic.

We followed the crowd, which conducted us to the other extremity of the wood, into an immenfe and verdant Amphitheatre, furrounded by the fineft trees I yet had feen. The profpect was charming, the trees were all hung with garlands of flowers, while a dozen neat cradles difperfed here and there, and fufpended with ribands to the large branches, were not, as you will find, the leaft interefting ornament of this delightful place.

My companion fhewed me the *Fir, Peter Novorgéve.* I admired its prodigious height, and fee-

ing

ing two oaks at fome diftance, between which
was placed a column of white marble upon a
hillock of earth, I afked my Guide what it meant.
I was anfwered, that thofe trees were particularly dear to Novorgêve; that one of them
bore the name of his father, the other of his
grandfather; and that the column was a monument of his tendernefs and refpect for their memories. On it was engraved a Ruffian infcription, which contained the eulogium of Anaftafius
and Alexis Novorgêve, dictated by feeling and
truth, of which the following is the fenfe:

" Heaven, in recompenfe of their fincere piety,
" taught them true happinefs; they found and en-
" joyed it in their family, in the pleafures of the
" country, and the labours of agriculture."

I fuppofe, continued I, that the cradle which I
obferve is more ornamented than the others, and
hung between thefe two oaks, is defigned for the
new-born infant.

Exactly fo; and look, the old man approaches
towards thofe trees: he takes the child, and places it
in the cradle.

Novorgêve having laid his grandfon in the
deftined place, formed a fpecies of trophy, compofed of various inftruments of hufbandry, which
were prefented to him, and which he attatched to
one of the trees by the fide of the cradle. He himfelf
explained the meaning of this cuftom, faying the

B 5

boy

boy was confecrated to the occupations of a
country life, and ended by reading aloud the infcription of the marble column.

When the old man had ceafed fpeaking, the
women, who had young children in their arms,
laid them in the other cradles, fat themfelves
down at the foot of the trees, took hold of long
ribands that hung from their fides, and pulling
them gently from time to time, gave an eafy motion to the cradles, thus balanced, and this way
amufed or fent the children to fleep (*a*). While
young mothers of twenty, in the midft of feafting,
found no pleafures fo fweet as thofe of tending
their children, the lads and laffes of the family
and the neighbourhood, affembled in their Amphitheatre, danced and fung in honour of the feaft.
They fung alfo a long ballad, entitled "The Seafons,"
in which, after having painted the pleafures of
Spring, of Summer, and of Autumn, they celebrated the Winter with ftill more circumftantial
energy; defcribed the fwiftnefs of their fledges,
and vaunted, in a fimple yet affecting manner, of
their long wintry evening, which glided fo de-
licioufly away, when affembled and fitting amidft
their families around their paternal fires.

(*a*) The country women in Ruffia, fufpend cradles
to trees during fummer, and rock their children after this
manner. See Les Coftumes Ruffes, by M. le Prince.

The

The fongs ended, they danced to the found of the Balayes (*a*), while feveral young girls walked round with bafkets, and offered the fpectators cakes and clougwa (*b*). The relations and neighbours took leave of the old man at noon and departed; but he detained me and my friend to dinner, and took us to the cottage which his father had formerly inhabited.

This place, faid he, retraces to my memory the moft pleafing ideas: here I come and meditate every morning; and, could it have contained my numerous family, here, beneath this revered roof, I had ended my days.

The old man then fat himfelf down upon a mat, and placed us by his fide. He fpoke French tolerably well, and anfwered my queftions with all the politenefs of a man who had lived twenty years at Court, and all the candour, good-nature, and fimplicity of a Hermit and a Hufbandman. He painted his happinefs in a moft affecting manner. I have known the Court, faid he, and all the pleafures which fuccefs, vanity, and favour can give; but then my head was bufy, and my heart was void and diffatisfied. A prey to inquietude and fear, I was obliged to defend myfelf from the

(*a*) A kind of guittar with a long neck.

(*b*) A nice fruit, fmaller than the cherry, and very common in Ruffia.

fnares

ſnares of hatred, and the malignily of envy, as
well as to ſupport the fatigue of indiſcreet re-
queſts. Each day I underwent the chagrin of making people diſcontented or ungrateful, and of ſeeing myſelf deprived of the counſels and conſola-
tions of friendſhip. Heaven, at length, removed
the film from my eyes, and taught me, that man,
ſent for a moment into exiſtence, is but a lunatic
to waſte that moment in accumulating periſhable
riches, and ſacrificing repoſe to cupidity. I loſt
half my fortune by giving up my employments;
but I recovered my freedom by renouncing facti-
titious paſſions: by again acquiring a taſte for the
pleaſures which nature preſents, I once more re-
gained the health I had loſt, and the pure happi-
neſs my early youth had known. Thus it is that
a ſimplicity of manners, occupations, and pleaſures, prolongs and embelliſhes life, and renders
our latter days as ſmiling and as fortunate as the
happy years of infancy; of which we preſerve ſo
powerful and ſo ſweet a recollection, only becauſe
they were ſpent in innocence, and free from the
tumults of the paſſions.

I was far from being tired of liſtening to the
virtuous Novorgêve, but dinner interrupted our
converſation. We ſat down to dinner in the
centre of the Amphitheatre where they had
danced. I beheld with rapture the old man ſurrounded by his family, and ſeated between his two
                                        reſpectable

refpectable Sifters. I could not underftand the language of his children, but I could fee the expreffion of their countenances, which internal joy and content infpired.

After dinner Novorgéve led me to his manfion, which was as fimple as it was vaft. No ftudied appendages of luxury and idlenefs; beds without curtains, wooden chairs and tables, and mats made of rufhes, compofed the furniture; long branches of trees artfully interlaced, and abundant in foliage, were the only ornaments (a).

The hall was large enough to contain all the family. Here they converfed about an hour, and then departed. We ftaid with the mafter of the houfe, who afked us to walk in his gardens; when we came there, he took off his order of Saint Andrew, hung it upon a tree, flung his coat upon the grafs, and taking a hoe, began to work, without interrupting his converfation with us.

The gardens were immenfe; I faw about a dozen Gardeners, and foon knew them to be the fons of Novorgéve, with whom we had dined. I then learnt, that the others were gone to fimilar

(a) It is the cuftom in Ruffia during fummer, and efpecially among the country people, thus to decorate the infide of their houfes; therefore it is, that fuch a quantity of people are met in their towns, loaded with green boughs to fell: in fome apartments, thefe branches are put in vafes full of water.   .

labours

labours in the adjacent fields, and that the women were all occupied in their houshold duties; some had the care of the kitchen, others of the dairy; some were spinning, some knitting, some sewing, not one was idle till seven o'clock in the evening, at which hour all the company assembled to supper. With what pleasure did they sit down! With what appetite did they eat!

Before they went to bed, the good Novorgêve read his children a moral and christian lesson; after which they all kneeled down, and the old man recited his prayers aloud, which he ended by pronouncing a benediction on the family. After this every body went to rest, and enjoyed the sweets of peaceable and profound sleep. The next morning I departed with a picture of this mansion, and of the happy Philosopher that owned it, which Time can never efface from my memory or my heart.

M. de la Paliniére ended, and the Baronnefs rose, thanked him for his complaisance, and instantly retired, for it was near half past ten o'clock. Their tales were interrupted for some days, because Madame de Clémire, whose turn it was to relate, had a cold; but they conversed together.

Cæsar recollected, that the Baronnefs, in her history of Olympia, had said honour was more severe than the laws; and asked the reason why?

The

The laws, replied the Baronnefs, are enacted for the general community; we muſt not expect generous and delicate fentiments from the multitude, confequently the laws cannot regulate certain actions and fenſations : were they more fevere, they would be obferved only by a few, therefore could not contribute to the general good: they confine themſelves to forbid manifeſt violence and injuſtice, becauſe they are made for the regulation of common and not fuperior minds. For which reaſon you may obferve, that the man whofe probity confiſts in merely obeying the laws, can neither be truly virtuous nor eſtimable; for he will find many opportunities of doing contemptible and even diſhoneſt acts, which the laws cannot puniſh. Hence you may comprehend, how law may authorize what honour may profcribe ; and wherefore it is ſhameful to profecute, in inſtances where you would be certain of gaining the cauſe.

But what is yet more, faid M. de la Paliniére, there are even crimes which, not having produced any tragical event, are not puniſhable by the laws: fuch for example as calumny (a).

But

(a) Calumniators in Poland are puniſhed in a way as odd as it is infamous to the Culprit ; when convicted, he is obliged, in full fenate, to crouch on the ground at the foot

But a Calumniator, faid Cæfar, is univerfally defpifed.

Certainly; he is difhonoured, and fo are all thofe who profit by the indulgence of the laws to commit acts, which are in themfelves unwarrantable.

I do not thoroughly comprehend, faid Cæfar, what you mean by being difhonoured?

A man whom the public voice accufes of difhonourable actions.

The multitude then has delicacy, fince its judgments are fo juft, and more fevere than the laws. Wherefore, *Law made for the multitude* ought to ordain virtuous acts.

There is no man, however wicked, or however vulgar, but what naturally loves virtue, and hates vice. His paffions make him act againft his confcience; but while his confcience reproves him for his own errors, it demonftrates fo clearly the errors of others, that he cannot reject its teftimony. Hence it is that men act ill, and judge well. Feeble, and corrupted, they give way

foot of the perfon's feat whofe honour he has attacked, and fay, with a loud voice, that when he fpread thefe injurious reports, *he lied like a dog.* After which public confeffion, he is obliged, three feveral times, to imitate the barking of a dog. This kind of punifhment is ftill practifed in Poland. *Hiftoire Général de Pologne, by M. le Chevalier de Solignac,* Tom. III.

to their paffions; but when they are cool, that is to fay, when they are unintereſted, they inſtantly condemn what they have often been guilty of; they revolt againſt every thing contemptible, they admire every thing generous, and they are moved at every thing affecting.

A bad father, or an ungrateful ſon, could not unaffectedly behold the aged mother of Angel-Sound bleſſing her children, and her great great-grand-children, or our good old Novorgêve, at the head of his family. They would admire pictures ſo ſublime, yet would feel no temptation to imitate like examples. Would they then obey a law which commanded them ſo to do? Such is the multitude, ſuch are men in general.——The moſt important concluſion that can be drawn from theſe reflections is, that every voice is raiſed to declaim againſt wickedneſs, and to praiſe virtue. Wherefore if we think reputation and general eſteem deſirable, to acquire them, we muſt be conſtantly good, worthy, and noble.

I have a queſtion to aſk, likewiſe, ſaid Caroline, concerning a word, the ſignification of which I do not well underſtand. Pray what do you mean when you ſpeak of prejudices (a)?

A pre-

(a) The explanation of the word prejudice here given by Madame de Genlis, as the reader will eaſily perceive,

is

A prejudice is an opinion formed without due reflection, and which cannot be supported by any good reasons: thus, for example, Mademoiselle Victoire believes that a bit of the rope, with which a man has been hanged, carried in her pocket, will make her win at cards. This is a prejudice, for it certainly is not the effect of reasoning, or the possibility of the fact, which could first make her give into such a belief. Ask her why she has this opinion, and she will tell you she had it of her aunt, her mother, or her grandmother, and that is all she knows.

All prejudices are not equally stupid with this; but I know many which I think so, and which yet are generally adopted. I have seen women fly frightened at the entrance of a person who nursed another sick of the small-pox or the measles; and I have seen these same women, with great tranquility, shut themselves up with the Physician who attended those very Patients. Many other things, of a like kind, may be observed, equally rational with Mademoiselle Victoire's predilection for the Hangman's rope.

is not strictly comformable to the English usage of that word; but as it may be so understood in English, without any great impropriety, it was thought best to retain the Author's own term. T.

But

But there is another species of prejudice, which, far from being ridiculous, deserves to be respected, because it is produced by a lively and delicate sensibility. Let us continue to believe that twins are united in perfect friendship; that they reciprocally suffer the bodily evils of each other; that a mother would discover her child whom she had never seen amidst a thousand other children; these are the errors of kind hearts, the consequences of virtuous sentiments, and ought not to be despised.

All opinions, which cannot be maintained by reason, and which facts and experiments demonstrate to be false, are certainly prejudices; but yet we must be careful how we affirm that any thing, with the nature of which we are unacquainted, however strange it may appear to us, is chimerical and vain. The history of Alphonso has taught us, that there exists an infinity of phænomena in Nature, the causes of which are unknown to man; for which reason we ought only to call those things prejudices, which are not only repugnant to reason, but which are capable of being proved false by facts.

I comprehend very well, mamma, at present, what is meant by prejudices; and, likewise, that all those which are not the effect of sensibility are ridiculous; such as the belief that Friday is an unfortunate day, that it is ill luck to spill salt, &c.

I hope

I hope you underftand, too, that any thing which religion, law, or honour ordains, cannot be called a prejudice.

O certainly!——Is the refpect that is paid to the dead and their tombs a prejudice?

No; becaufe religion ordains us to honour them, and becaufe the rites of burial are holy.

That is true. But fhould our refpect for the dead extend ar far as is commonly thought, when people fay, that it is a lefs crime to fpeak ill of the living than of the dead?

The queftion embarraffes me!——Let us confult a fure guide on this fubject; Religion. Does it command us.to refpect the memory of thofe that are gone, more than of thofe that remain?

It certainly does not, faid the Baronnefs; it commands us to love our neighbour as our felf, and render him good for evil (a). Surely, there-fore, it is more wicked to take away the reputa-tion of the living, than to attack the memory of the dead.

Befides that, the dead hear not, feel not, while the living are driven to defpair; for which reafon, that opinion muft be a prejudice, as has been fhewn: for, if, for inftance, a perfon fhould feek,

(a) Blefs them which perfecute you; blefs, and curfe not.—Dearly beloved, avenge not yourfelves, but rather give place unto wrath; for it is written, vengeance is mine, I will repay faith the Lord.—Rom. xii. 14, 19.

after

after the death of his enemy, to injure his memory
by new and vague accufations, he would add
meannefs to malice, becaufe that, the dead cannot
anfwer, cannot defend his reputation. Were he
living, he might clear up conjecture, and prove
the falfity of what remained in doubt; but he
could not deny eftablifhed facts: and this is the
reafon, why an accufation, founded only on fuf-
picion, is fo unworthy an act.

I would have you, however, underftand I not
only difapprove, but deteft a fenfelefs animofity
againft the dead, although they are infenfible to
wrongs. My intention was only to fhew, there is
much lefs cruelty in attacking the memory of the
dead than of the living.

I will remember what you have told me, mamma,
faid Caroline.

Two days after this converfation, Madame de
Clémire being alone with Caroline, faid to her,
when I came into your bedchamber this morning,
my dear, I faw one of the maids buckling your
fhoes. How could you fuffer this? To debafe a
fellow-creature is to debafe yourfelf. You never
fhould require any thing of a fervant except fuch
affiftance as is abfolutely neceffary to you; but
avoid as much as poffible whatever gives trouble,
or can infpire repugnance. Never bafely and cru-
elly take advantage of your fituation, and refufe the
refpect due to all; but if you wifh to be refpected
yourfelf,

yourself, accuftom yourfelf betimes to revere in others the facred rights of humanity.

I cannot drefs myfelf entirely alone, therefore my maid affifts to lace me, comb up my hair, and fo forth; but I can undrefs myfelf, and I have never, fince I have been married, made my fervant fit up for that purpofe, but have gone to bed without her aid. I have lived in the fafhionable world, have been at balls, have come home at four and five o'clock in the morning with all the paraphernalia of drefs, loaded with flowers and pins, almoft innumerable, of which it was no eafy tafk to get rid; but I a thoufand times preferred the taking of this trouble, and going to bed fomewhat later, to the alternative of receiving help from an unfortunate wretch half afleep, and out of temper; who, while fhe undreffed me, would fecretly curfe my pleafures and her own condition. At prefent I have little merit in undreffing myfelf, becaufe the ornaments of Champcery are fimple, and foon thrown off. ——

You never ring your bell in the night I obferve, mamma.

Never; unlefs I am ill. If I am gone to bed, and want any thing, I rife and get it myfelf, even in the depth of winter; and this I am fo accuftomed to, that I never get cold; but have acquired an activity which I believe to be very

healthy,

healthy, for nothing enfeebles the body like idlenefs and effeminacy. Such habits beget addrefs,
ftrength, and agility. I have by no means a ro-
buft appearance, and yet I every evening perform
acts of real force; I can carry a huge pitcher
of water, and in winter continually put large
logs upon the fire much heavier than myfelf.

I wifh to imitate you, mamma; and henceforth,
if you will permit me, I will always undrefs myfelf

No, you are too young at prefent; your's is
the age of feeblenefs and dependence; but even
now, you may help yourfelf much oftener than
you do; and hereafter you will be very wife, to
acquire the habits I have defcribed.

I promife you, mamma, no more to treat fer-
vants with a want of proper refpect.

The attention we fhould pay them is, perhaps, greater than you imagine. You ought to be
careful not to fpeak any thing directly or indirectly
that could make them afhamed of their condition.
Thus it would be inexpreffibly cruel to make ufe
of the proverb *He lies like a Lackey*, in prefence of
a footman : it becomes us carefully to avoid
fuch rudenefs, fince, while it humiliates, it excites refentment and hatred. We ought, likewife, to be exceedingly circumfpect in all our
words and actions when they are prefent; fince
the

the impreffion they receive, from obferving their fuperiors, has the greateft effect upon their manners : we fhould, therefore, be doubly guilty in giving them bad examples. In fine, Religion, Juftice, Humanity, all equally require us to treat them with gentlenefs and indulgence ; to endeavour to promote their interefts, to protect them on all juft occafions, and affectionately to affift them when they are ill, or have become old in our fervice.

Madame de Clémire was going to rife and take a walk, but was ftopt by Caroline, who faid fhe had fomething more to confide to her. She then confeffed, that during the morning fhe had been a little ill-tempered with Pulcheria.

You have, no doubt, repaired the wrong you did her, faid Madame de Clémire ?

Yes, mamma, replied Caroline ; though I did myfelf fome violence, I refolved to overcome my ill humour, and all the reft of the morning we were as good friends as ever.

And did not you make an apology ? Did not you regret your having been unjuft, though but for a moment ?

As foon as fhe faw me good tempered fhe was fo too, and did not feem to be vexed the leaft in the world. .

But

But becaufe fhe did not bear malice, muft you appear infenfible of her generofity? If I had ill treated the loweft fervant in the houfe, I would fhew him I was forry for it; and by fo doing, fhould think I did honour to myfelf; for nothing elevates us more than equity: the greateft defect a perfon can have, is that of knowing, yet not acknowledging themfelves to be wrong. The imperfection of our nature is fuch, that fcarce a day can pafs, in which we have not committed fome error; for which reafon the people moft amiable, and moft beloved, will always be thofe who, by confeffing the wrongs they have done, fhew their candour and goodnefs of heart. This fublime quality always appertains to the generous and the feeling; while little and confined minds, enflaved by falfe fhame, as mean as it is foolifh, would rather aggravate their faults than retract them, or fay a word in expiation.

I will run and feek my fifter, mamma, and make an apology to her for being out of temper, and for not having fhewn I was forry I had been fo.

This procured Caroline a tender kifs, and fhe immediately left the room, running to find her fifter.

Madame de Clémire had promifed in the morning fhe would tell them a fhort ftory after fupper, and in the evening fhe thus acquitted herfelf of her promife.

THE

SOLITARY FAMILY

OF

NORMANDY.

A FEW leagues from Forges (*a*), near the rich Abbey of Bobec, and in the province of Normandy, lived a good Farmer, whofe name was Anfelmo, with his wife and children. He was poor, but fo happy, that he had never left his houfe but to go to church. His little habitation ftood by itfelf in the midft of a foreft; he had no neighbours, and he wifhed for none; for he could not imagine, after he had been all day labouring in his field, it was poffible to find a pleafure more fweet than that of repofing in the midft of his family.

(*a*) Forges is 26 leagues from Paris, and celebrated for its Mineral Waters.

Three

Three acres of land, two cows, and a little poultry, were the whole of his riches; he had no other fociety but that of his wife and five children, a fervant maid, and a herdfman, with whom it is neceffary you fhould become better acquainted.

The maid's name was Jacquelina. She had been bred in the houfe of Anfelmo, and had acquired the manner, and fedentary habits of the family; fhe had never been above half a league from the houfe. Of all the edifices which cover the earth, fhe knew none but the Cottage of Anfelmo, and the Abbey of Bobec; and never did St. Peter's at Rome, or the Colonade of the Louvre, excite greater admiration, than the little church of Bobec gave Jacquelina.

She had heard fpeak of Forges, but hearing that it was four leagues off, fhe never could be tempted to undertake fo long a journey. Jacquelina, as you may imagine, could not read; fhe had never feen a book in her life, except at church. Her talents were confined to the milking of cows, the making of cheefe, and aiding her miftrefs in houfhold duties. Her mind was not capable of any extenfive knowledge; fhe had pre-cifely that degree of intelligence, neceffary to tolerably fulfil the duties of her condition; and if Heaven had not fent her rulers as patient as

they

they were humane, she would more than once have been liable to lose her place.

She committed no voluntary faults, however; it was want of memory and reflection only; for her intentions were so upright, and her heart so good, that Anselmo and his wife never could resolve to scold her.

The Herdsman, Michael, who kept the cows, was still less active and less intelligent than Jacquelina; but, in the eyes of the indulgent Anselmo, the weakness of his constitution excused his indolence and incapacity; besides, Michael was naturally gentle, peaceable, honest, and so patient, that it was not possible to make him angry.

There was so much conformity between Michael and Jacquelina, that it would have been a miracle, being, as they were, always together, had they not formed an attachment to each other. Sympathy declared itself, and the two lovers asked permission to marry, which was easily granted. Michael wedded Jacquelina, and, in three years time, was the father of three children, who were all brought up with the children of Anselmo.

About this time, Jacquelina, patient as she was, underwent great trouble. The wife of Anselmo died. Neither did the good man survive her above two years; by which accident, Michael and Jacquelina lost the best of masters, and the sole sup-

port

port they had upon earth. The relations, who
were left Guardians of the children, came to
occupy the little heritage, and had the cruelty to
turn away Michael and Jacquelina.

They were obliged to quit the cherished cottage which they regarded as their paternal manfion, and to tear themselves from the arms of the
virtuous Anfelmo's children, who, for the laſt two
years, had called Jacquelina by the kind name of
mother. The poor woman wept over them, and
left them in defpair, followed by four of her own
children, and the mournful Michael, who carried
under his arm a large bundle of coarſe cloathing,
which contained all the riches of this unfortunate
family.

It was happy for them, that in this dreadful
fituation, they felt none of thoſe diſtraching in-
quietudes which forethought and fancy give; their
forrows were only the forrows of a moment; the
future was to them hid by a veil ſo thick, they
even could not form an image of the morrow.
They had dined well before they left their old habitation, and were not much diſturbed about where
they ſhould ſup; all their converſation was regret
for the death of Anfelmo, and tendernefs for the
children they had been obliged to abandon.

Converſing ſimply thus, they followed where-
ever chance pleaſed to lead, till they had loſt them-

ſelves

felves in the foreft. Jacquelina was fix months gone with child, and being fatigued, refted herfelf at the foot of a tree. Her hufband fat himfelf down by her fide, and the four children ranged themfelves around.

It was in the month of July, and, as day began to decline, one of the children faid he was hungry, and all the reft immediately afked for bread. Michael had fome provifions in his wallet, which he partook with his wife and children. After fupper, they determined to pafs the night in the wood; and at break of day they found a beaten path, which brought them into a kind of wildernefs, on the outfide of the foreft. This wild place was full of broom, and they found a ftream of pure water, which ran from a rock covered with mofs, the fight of which gave Jacquelina great joy. Still to increafe their happinefs, along the fkirts of the foreft, they found plenty of nuts, mulberries, and wild rafberries, with an infinity of ftrawberries.

Jacquelina was quite enchanted at this garden of Nature. Oh Michael! cried fhe, let us always live here; for look you, there is water, and here are fruits, and they will be fufficient for us; let us make a Hut of the branches of trees, to keep out the rain.——It juft then occurred to the mind of Jacquelina, that they muft firft have leave to lop

the

the trees, and the reflection made her forrowful.
At this moment fhe perceived a young Peafant, at
fome diftance, gathering ftrawberries: to him fhe
went, and afked if he knew to whom the place
where they were belonged?——

Yes, to the Abbey of Bobec, replied the Peafant.

Are we far from the Abbey?

Three quarters of a league; I am going there
prefently, with the ftrawberries I have gathered.

Jacquelina then went and advifed with her hufband; and Michael, having received her inftructions, departed with the young Peafant to the
Abbey of Bobec, leaving Jacquelina with his
children at the entrance of the foreft, and promifed to return as foon as poffible.

Arrived at the Abbey, Michael obtained a moment's audience of the Abbot, to whom he related his fituation; he ended by afking work, or
at leaft permiffion to eftablifh himfelf in the place
where he had left his family.

What can you do, faid the Abbot?

Keep cows.

We have no need of Herdfmen; befides, you
do not belong to our diftrict,

But I have no means of a livelihood, and that
is all the fame.

Alas! we cannot relieve all the poor.

I am

I am not poor; I afk no alms; our hearts are willing, and we can work.

You can do nothing; befides I tell you, that the inhabitants of our own diftrict muft have the preference.

But I am very weak and fickly, I affure you, and fo you ought to take me into your fervice.

What becaufe you are incapable of working?

Yes to be fure; it was for that reafon that my dead mafter Anfelmo took me into his fervice, and would never turn me away; but if you do not like fickly people, at leaft, Mr. Abbot, give us leave to build a little hut with boughs, upon the heath.

How will you live there?

With wild fruits and roots; there are water-creffes, ftrawberries, nuts, water.——Truly it is a paradife.

What will you do in winter?

Winter!——We never thought of winter; but winter will not be here fo foon, this is only July.

Hark you, good man, fince you are fo very defirous of it, I permit you to build your Hut; and moreover, I authorife you to come every other day to the Abbey, for a fupply of bread and potatoes for you and your family.

I have a wallet.

Go,

Go, that is all I can do for you.

Oh! that is more than I afked——Jacquelina will be fo happy!

· Michael haftily departed, and was already at fome little diftance, when they called him back, by the order of the Abbot, to give him brown bread and potatoes roafted in the afhes. Michael, who was truly honeft, refufed at firft to receive them.——The Abbot told me, faid he, I was only to come every other day, fo I will come for them the day after to-morrow.

In fpite of his refiftance, however, they filled his pockets and hands with the provifions deftined for two days, and he departed, highly fatisfied with the fuccefs of his journey. He found Jacquelina, came up to her with a triumphant air, and anfwered all her queftions. Jacquelina, though quite happy at the recital, fcolded him a little notwithftanding, for not having bought an axe, in the village of Bobec, to cut down the branches ; for, faid fhe, here we have feven fhillings and eleven-pence, (it was the fruit of ten years favings) and what are we to do with all that money ?

That is true, replied Michael, but one cannot think of every thing ; we had forgot, you know, that winter would come..

Oh!

Oh! now you mention winter, you muſt keep the money to buy ſheeps ſkins, that we may lie comfortably.

Ay, ſo I will; we will have every thing comfortable I warrant, ſince we are to live here.

Come, let us go to work, we can cut the ſmall branches with our knives.

Jacquelina went towards the wood, her huſband followed, and they worked till night. The huſband and the wife were neither of them robuſt or active, for which reaſon they were a fortnight in conſtructing their Hut; which was tolerably ſolid it is true, but which had one inconvenience unperceived by them, till their work was almoſt finiſhed. They had forgot; for, as Michael ſaid, they could not think of every thing, that they were to live in the Hut, and that conſequently it was neceſſary it ſhould be as high as themſelves. It is eaſier to work within your reach, than to clamber and raiſe your arms above your head, and they did what would give them the leaſt trouble.

Jacquelina and Michael could lean upon their Hut, as you would lean upon a balcony. Jacquelina was the firſt who remarked this defect of conſtruction, and though the building was far advanced, had ſo much fortitude as to be tempted to begin the work again, had not Michael perſuaded her to.

the

the contrary; for, faid he, people do not want a houfe, except to reft in, and we can either fit or lie down in ours.

Jacquelina had nothing to anfwer to this reafoning, and notwithftanding its erroneous dimenfions, the Hut was finifhed.

The day on which they dined in it, for the firft time, was a holiday; Michael had been, in the morning, to the Abbey, whence he had brought potatoes and frefh bread, and likewife a pint of milk and fome eggs, which he had purchafed in the village. The joy of the children was exceffive at the fight of this delicious feaft, and their gaiety excited that of Michael and Jacquelina, fo that nothing was wanting to the happinefs of the banquet, for the guefts had good appetites and good humour; and when night came, found fleep and tranquility came alfo. After having paffed above eight and twenty nights expofed to the injuries of the open air, they found an inexpreffible fatisfaction in lying down beneath a thick foliage, and on frefh ftraw; in the morning they awaked in the moft perfect health.

There is nothing fo comfortable, faid Michael, as to have every thing at one's eafe. They may well fay, that ufe makes all things eafy; yet I fhould never have flept fo well upon the ground, and with the fkies for a covering.

Nor

Nor I neither, replied Jacquelina; I always thought of the warm stable, where we lay when our good dear master was alive.

Our Hut though is quite as good as the stable, Jacquelina.

Oh certainly; and now we have a house, we ought always to be happy at home, as our good master used to say.

Michael the evening before had bought a platter, five wooden spoons, several warm sheep's skins, and some flax for Jacquelina, who had a distaff, and could spin tolerably; and thus it was, that he had expended his seven shillings and elevenpence. Michael on his part, found means of employing himself; he caught birds with birdlime, which he carried to the Abbey; and in a month's time he went to sell his wife's work, which did not come to much: for as I have said, Jacquelina was neither active nor industrious.

The summer glided away, and in the month of September Jacquelina was happily delivered of a little daughter. Winter at last arrived, and notwithstanding their sheeps skins, their Hut did not seem half so agreeable; nor could they find either rasberries, bilberries, or other wild fruits.

Michael and Jacquelina, however, suffered much less from the cold than might be supposed; they had never in their lives slept in a close chamber,

ber, in which there was a chimney; the ftable, which they remembered with fo much affection, was open in the roof in feveral places, and had various fractures in its fides, large enough to put the hand through; fo that Jacquelina and her hufband found no great difference, even during the rigours of winter, between the Hut and the ftable they regretted; and in fummer, their Hut, being fituated on a healthy foil, and fheltered by a foreft, in which grew multitudes of herbs, flowers, and fruits, was much more agreeable than a gloomy damp ftable, built in a yard, furrounded by dung, and in which was a great pond of green ftagnant water.

Towards the end of winter Michael, who for the laft two months could hardly walk as far as the Abbey, at laft found it impoffible to go thither and receive their fubfiftence. Jacquelina therefore went in his ftead, and poor Michael was obliged to ftay in his Hut, gloomily extended on dry leaves. He did not fuffer any great pain; and his natural piety and tranquillity, preferved him from laffitude and impatience: he prayed to God all the day, and Jacquelina fpun and told her beads by his fide: his children continually came to carefs him, fo that he could not abfolutely be called miferable; and a year paft away in this manner.

Michael

Michael and Jacquelina had lived two years in their Hut, when one day (it was the month of July) Jacquelina, who had been gathering fruits round the foreſt, came running, quite out of breath. Oh Michael, cried ſhe, you cannot think what a fine thing I have juſt ſeen!

Ay, what?

Oh dear! a coach without a top; it is made for all the world like a cart; but then it is all yellow, and ſhines ſo——beſides it is drawn by ſix horſes all over ſilver——and there are ſuch fine ladies in the coach, and ſuch fine gentlemen behind, with coats as red as our Billy's cheeks—— And——

Jacquelina heard the noiſe of the landau which ſhe had been deſcribing; her heart beat with joy, ſhe ran from her Hut, and all her little ones followed her. The landau was not thirty paces from her; in it, ſuperior to all the reſt, was one angelic lady, who, looking at her and her children with gentle ſmiles, ordered the coachman to ſtop.

Jacquelina, ſurprized and aſtoniſhed, durſt not advance, whilſt the young and beauteous ſtranger, followed by four ladies, who alighted with her from the carriage, approached.——Are theſe five children all your's? ſaid ſhe.

Yes, my lady.

Poor .

Poor little creatures! Why they are almoſt naked.

Oh! the three youngeſt have jackets, but we keep them againſt winter.

And do you live all day in this Hut?

Yes, my lady, and all night too.

What, have you no other dwelling?

No, my lady; we have not had for theſe two years paſt. We live very well in the ſummer; but to be ſure it is a little cold in the winter: eſpecially ſince my huſband has been ill.

Your huſband ill! and lying in that Hut!

Yes, my lady.

Merciful Providence!——How happy am I we have loſt our way, and that Chance has conducted us hither.

The angelic ſtranger went towards the Hut, and with her attendants endeavoured to enter; but their high heeled ſhoes, and their hats and feathers, obliged them to ſtoop ſo much, that the ſtranger, unable to ſupport the pain of ſuch an attitude, kneeled down in the Hut.——Good God! ſaid ſhe, turning her tearful eyes on Michael, and have you had no other aſylum than this for two years?——Could you find no relief at Forges?

Forges is ſo far off, my lady!

It is but three leagues.

My

My husband has been sickly this year and a half, and I could not leave him to undertake so long a journey; besides we have wanted for nothing, they have always given us bread and potatoes at the Abbey.

The stranger took out her purse: take these, said she to Jacquelina. I will send for you this evening; but since you love this place so much, I promise you shall return again. I only desire you to pass some time at Forges, for your husband wants the assistance of a Physician.

While the stranger was speaking, Jacquelina was considering the pieces of gold the stranger had given her.——Since you are so very good my lady, said she, I must make bold to tell you, that these pieces you have given me will do us no good; they do not know what they are in this country.

What, have you never seen gold?

Oh yes, my lady, to be sure I have seen the gilding in the church at Bobec; but as for golden money I never heard speak of any such thing, and I am sure nobody will take it.

The stranger, struck by an excess of poverty, of which she had never before had an idea, could not retain her tears; she prevailed, however, on Jacquelina to keep the gold she had received; but for her better satisfaction she gave her some crown pieces, which were received with gratitude and

joy.

joy. After which, she and her attendants left the Hut, remounted their carriage, and returned to Forges, leaving Michael and Jacquelina aftonished and tranſported.

They talked of nothing but the beautiful lady; and their converſation was ſtill on the ſame ſubject, when the Meſſengers arrived to take them to Forges. Four men carefully placed Michael on a kind of bier, on which he was carried lying on a mattreſs. Jacquelina and her children were ſeated in a covered cart; and our little troop arrived at Forges about nine o'clock in the evening.

They were conducted to a houſe, where they found clean linen and good beds. As ſoon as Michael was put to bed, Jacquelina ran to interrogate her hoſteſs, and in leſs than half an hour returned.——Oh Michael, ſaid ſhe, thou wilt be ſo ſurprized!——That beautious lady——Doſt thou know what a Princeſs is?

No, truly.

Well, that fine lady is a Princeſs!——And moreover ſhe is called a Ducheſs——and beſides all which, ſhe has another name ſtill——But that I have forgot; however, what is moſt of all, ſhe is——Ay, ſhe is a relation to the King!

How can that be? She has no pride!

No more ſhe has, as thou ſayeſt.

How

How can a relation of the King's have such mildness in her looks, and such gentleness in her words?

Thou wilt never guess what she is come to Forges for!——It is to drink of a certain water here that makes women have children; for my share, I have no opinion about any such water; but I will say my prayers once a day the oftener for her, that God may give this dear good lady as many children as her heart could wish, that so she may be happy,

Their conversation was interrupted by the Hostess, who brought them an excellent supper. Michael and his wife had before time drank bad cyder, but never any sort of wine, and, for the first time in their lives, they tasted it to the health of their benefactress. After which Jacquelina went to bed, thanking God, and pouring forth a thousand blessings on her young and virtuous Protectress.

On the morrow Jacquelina was awakened by a woman, who came to tell her, the Princess had ordered her to take measure of her and her children, and make shifts and clothes for all the family. Accordingly some days after, Jacquelina received all kinds of necessaries; shoes, stockings, caps, nothing was forgotten.

Jacquelina's joy was so much the greater, for that her husband's health was presently re-esta-
blished.

blifhed. The affiduous cares of the Phyfician, a
healthy lodging, and good food, foon produced a
furprifing alteration, and in three weeks time he
was able to rife and walk about his chamber.

At this epocha, Jacquelina had an interview
with her benefactrefs, who prefented her with a
bunch of keys. There, faid fhe, are the keys of
your houfe, your clofets, and your cupboards;
return home my good Jacquelina, and to-morrow
morning I will come and breakfaft with you.
Jacquelina, aftonifhed at what fhe heard, ftuttered
a few words, and received the keys with a ftupid
air, thinking it impoffible that fhe could have
a houfe with cupboards and clofets, or that a
relation of the King's could come to breakfaft
with her.

The fame day Michael, his wife, and children
were reconducted to the wildernefs, where they had
been originally found; but what was their amaze-
ment when they faw, inftead of their former rude
Hut, a well-built little houfe, fituated in the midft
of a large garden. The children ran and danced
with joy, and Michael and Jacquelina kiffed and
wept over them.——Oh! my God, faid Jacquelina, clafping her hands, what have we done to deferve all this happinefs?

They entered their habitation, and found it
compofed of two good rooms, with a pile of
wood

wood at the end, and a little kitchen, well furnish-
ed with houshold utenfils ; there was a chimney in
the bedchamber, and for furniture they had two
good beds with ftrong curtains, two wooden tables,
four rufh-bottomed chairs, two armed chairs, and
a large prefs.

Jacquelina took her bunch of keys, opened her
prefs, and there found two complete fuits of clothes
for her hufband, and the fame for herfelf and children ; there were fhifts, ftockings, bonnets, and,
moreover, fheets and towels, and a large quantity
of flax to fpin.

As foon as fhe had taken an inventory of her
prefs, Jacquelina was brought into her garden,
already well fupplied with vegetables, and afterwards fhewn a hen-rooft, where were a fcore of
fowls.   At laft her Conductor opened the door of
an outhoufe, in which were two milch cows, and
informed her fhe was the owner of a fmall meadow,
about a quarter of a mile from the houfe.   Jacquelina thought herfelf in a dream.   What, faid fhe
to her hufband, are we richer than our dear good
mafter Anfelmo was? Why his cottage was but a
ftable, when compared to this——Our garden
too is twice as large——Oh Michael ! we muft
never forget our Hut, efpecially in the winter,
when with our children we fhall fit round our
fire ;

fire; for we ought always to thank God as fin-
cerely as we do at prefent.

While fhe fpoke thus, tears of joy dropt from the
eyes of Jacquelina; Michael alfo wept, and both
kiffed their children, who received their careffes
with a pleafure they had never felt before, though
they had been always tenderly beloved.

Jacquelina could not clofe her eyes all night;
fhe had a lamp upon the chimney-piece, and fhe
paffed the hours in contemplating, with admiration,
her chamber and her goods, and praying God to
blefs her illuftrious Benefactrefs.   At break of day
fhe rofe, and fo did Michael, and the happy couple
again went to vifit their kitchen, their garden,
their hen-rooft, and their cow-houfe.   They
afterwards dreffed their children, put on their beft
clothes, and prepared breakfaft; the table was
fpread with a napkin quite new, and furnifhed
with two large pans of cream, brown bread, frefh
butter, and a bafket of nuts juft gathered, after
which they waited for their dear good lady, with
equal anxiety and impatience.

At eleven o'clock their eldeft fon, who flood
fentinel at the wood-fide, quitted his poft, and
came running to announce the firft fight of the
landau.   Michael and Jacquelina, with beating
hearts, each took the child by the hand; and
Michael, who was yet far from being ftrong, was
forry

forry that he could not run fafter. The children foon outftript them, and ran tumultuoufly towards the carriage, while their father and mother in vain called to them to keep back.

Scarcely had Jacquelina and Michael got out of their yard-gate, before the young Princefs had alighted. They threw themfelves at her feet, bathed in tears; and Jacquelina, pointing to her hufband, with a faultering voice, faid, look, my deareft lady, look, he is quite well——He can run. Here too are our children, they will not complain of cold; and here is our houfe, where we fhall be. as happy in winter as in the fummer.——This is all your doing, and a righteous God only can reward you. As for us, alas! we do not know how to thank you.

A deluge of tears interrupted her fpeech, while the charming and virtuous Princefs wept in company, raifed Jacquelina, took hold of her arm, and entered the houfe. You may well fuppofe the breakfaft was thought excellent; that they walked afterwards in the garden, and that Michael and Jacquelina pointed out all their acquifitions and all their wealth.

The Princefs departed at one o'clock, and foon arrived at Forges; where fhe learnt with pleafure and emotion, that there is no condition, no clafs, in which the fame generous and fublime fentiments may not be found, as thofe by which fhe

was

was fo nobly diftinguifhed. The Mafons, who had built the houfe in the wildernefs, affected by an action which thus made a whole family happy, were defirous, as much as in them lay, of participating; they worked day and night at the building, and as foon as it was finifhed, unanimoufly refufed to accept the money offered in payment. It was impoffible to make them receive the leaft recompenfe; and there was no other way of rewarding, but by immediately employing them, about other jobs, for which they were paid double the fum they afked.

Madame de Clémire ceafing to fpeak, M. de la Paliniére exclaimed, this is a charming ftory. It is not difficult to divine the name of the auguft benefactrefs of Michael and Jacquelina (a); and indeed, fhe has done fo many things of the like kind, that this has not given me the leaft furprize; but the generofity of the Mafons aftonifhes me. It would be very extraordinary to find one man, in fuch a clafs of people, with fuch a greatnefs of foul; but that they fhould all agree to work day and night, for the fole pleafure of participating in a good action; that they fhould obftinately refufe the wages due to their labour, and that with one con-

(a) *The Duchefs de Chartres is undoubtedly meant. Madame, the Countefs de Genlis, has apartments in the Palais Royal.* T.

fent

sent they thus should sacrifice their time and trouble, themselves being all, poor, and blush to accept money so hardly earned; there is, I say, in this proceeding something so noble, so delicate, such an enthusiasm of virtue, as, I own, appears to me to have very little probability among people in so rude a state; and I confess, I am persuaded you have been imposed upon respecting this Anecdote.

But what would you say, if I myself had been a witness of the fact?

Is it possible! You delight me! For there is nothing I more ardently wish than to find it true.

We dare not invent incidents like this, because we have but an imperfect idea of the capabilities of nature. We would not acknowledge her in pictures of the imagination, were she painted in all her sublimity; for, by a capricious Inconsistency, the heroism which we admire in history, seems, in a work of invention, nothing but an extravagant fiction, devoid of all appearance of truth. Let me, however, observe, that what Critics call the imaginary sublime, has no real existence: for there is nothing the fancy can create, however generous, however noble, of which man is not capable, when he gives way to the first emotions of the mind, or is stimulated by great examples. Nay, the idea of constant perfection, such as we can conceive, do we not find it fulfilled,

when

when we examine the lives of thofe who fcrupuloufly practife all the duties and devoti ns of religion?

The Baronnefs made her Repeater ftrike, as
Madame de Clémire ended. It is not yet ten
o'clock, mamma, faid Cæfar, your ftory has been
too fhort; and then it ended fo fuddenly we had
not time to afk a fingle queftion.

True, faid Pulcheria; I, for my part, long to
know whether the prayers of Jacquelina fucceeded.

They did, anfwered Madame de Clémire; her
Benefactrefs became a Mother the year following;
I will tell you an Anecdote of a child fhe had.

This charming little girl is now fix years and
a half old; fhe lives in the country every fummer; and laft year, as fhe was walking in the
foreft of Montmorenci, fhe met a pretty little
country girl hand in hand with her mother;
the mother offered her bafket of ftrawberries to
the young Princefs, who coming nearer to the
little girl, perceived fhe was blind, at which fhe
was much furprized; for, at a diftance, the child
feemed to have very fine eyes. The woman was
queftioned, and replied, that the child was not
blind at her birth, but that fhe had not the means
to take her to Paris to the Surgeons.

Why, faid the Princefs, can the Surgeons re-
ftore her to fight?

So I am told.

Well then, I will take her to Paris myself, when I return thither; I will make room for her in the coach by my side.

The poor mother was much affected by this promise, and the attendants of the young Princess told her to come the next morning to her country-seat. Accordingly what the Princess had promised was performed; and as soon as they arrived at Paris, the little girl was immediately sent to the house of an Oculist, who kept her all the summer, and part of the winter. The next spring, when the young Princess returned into the country, they surprized her very agreeably, by bringing her the little Peasant perfectly recovered. What! cried she, are you no longer blind?

No, mademoiselle.

And are not you very glad?

'To be sure; I can work now.

And read too.

No, mademoiselle, I cannot read.

No! How does that happen? You are older than I am, and I can.

I have been two years blind.

That is true: but now you can see, and you may soon learn.

My mother cannot pay for my schooling.

Poor

Poor thing——Are you willing to learn from me? If it will give you any pleasure, I will teach you a lesson every day.

The little girl, at hearing this, thought the Princess was laughing at her, and began to laugh herself; but the Princess insisted she was in earnest, while one of her attendants apparently combated her resolution.——Recollect, mademoiselle, said she, that a teacher must have patience not to be moved.

I shall have that.

It will be so long before she has learned.

I shall not be tired; but I could read, when I had only had fifteen lessons.

You could so; and many children, by the same method, might be taught to read in as short a space of time (1): however, if Nanette should be slow at learning, or should want application, three months will not be sufficient to teach her.

Shall we be here three months?

Yes, mademoiselle.

Oh, then Nanette will have time enough.

So saying, this amiable child ran to seek her book, and her box of counters; then made Nanette sit down before her, and with the utmost gentleness and intelligence gave her a long lesson; after which the girl was suffered to depart, but desired to come again the next day at the same hour.

Though

Though Nanette, as had been predicted, was not very industrious, her mistress was not discouraged, but with a degree of patience and perseverance, very extraordinary at her age, accomplished what she had begun. It was a delightful sight to see her giving her lesson, pointing with her little fingers to the figures on the counters, and the words, reading aloud, prompting in a whisper, promising her scholar rewards, proud of her improvement, and, whenever she read well, looking round to collect the suffrages of the astonished spectators. This was one of those pleasing yet affecting pictures, which produce the most charming sensations in the heart, and of which it is impossible to tire.

Nanette, in fact, before the end of Autumn, had learnt to read almost as well as her young mistress, who gave her sweetmeats, clothes, and books; and when she parted with her, said, Good bye Nanette, next summer I will teach you something else.

Oh the charming little Princess! cried Pulcheria; she will be worthy of her mother. This reflection terminated the evening's conversation.

Before they went to bed, the children asked, and obtained leave, to go to the vintage of farmer Benoit; accordingly they rose next morning sooner than ordinary, to see if the Basket-maker

had

had sent home all the materials they had ordered above a fortnight ago.   At eight o'clock, four pretty back baskets were brought suitable to the height of Cæsar, his two sisters, and Augustine; four panniers with handles, and four pair of large scissars to cut the grape-stalks.

An hour after dinner, they set off on foot to the Vineyard of farmer Benoit, which was about half a league from the Castle; here it was agreed, this little company should work two full hours for the farmer; after which they should take their Nunchions, with the Grape-gatherers, and then fill their back baskets and their panniers, on their own account, and send them to the Castle by the cart; which agreements were faithfully observed, with great pleasure on both sides; and the farmer gave this glorious testimony, that his own children had not been more industrious than those of the Castle.   Never was day spent more agreeably, or seemed more amusing; they did not leave the Vineyard till the approach of night.

When they came to Champcery, Cæsar having a little out-stript the rest, entered the court-yard first: here he found the servants assembled round a horseman who had but just arrived; he heard them all speaking at once, and continually repeating the name of his father.   He quickened his pace, ran, and they made way for him, each

cages.

eager to tell him, that the Marquis de Clémire
was not above half a league off. Cæsar, quite
transported, ran to the Courier; he alighted,
Cæsar looked, and recollecting the Valet de
Chambre of his father, immediately jumped up,
embraced, and wept over him.

Madame de Clémire and his sisters were soon
there; they kissed each other a thousand times,
all weeping with joy. The Courier was questioned, the coach was called, the horses were put to
in an instant, away they went; in less than a
quarter of an hour the Postillions stopt, the coach-
doors flew open, and the dear father of the family,
after a year's absence, found himself in the arms of
his wife and children.

All the while they were in the coach together,
they could only express their transports by tears
and tender embraces. The night was dark, they
had no flambeaux, yet they were desirous of seeing
each other. No sooner did they enter the hall of
Champcery, than their transports and tenderness
were redoubled. The Marquis never could be
tired with looking at Cæsar and his dear little
girls. What father, after so long an absence,
does not find his children improved? The Marquis admired how much and how finely his were
grown.

On

On the other hand it was remarked, with inexpreffible fatisfaction, that the fatigues of war had produced no change in the appearance of the Marquis, but that he evidently enjoyed a perfect ftate of health.

They fat up till midnight, and in the morning the children rofe with the day; for the joy of the over-night, and their anxiety again to fee their father, had prevented them from fleeping. The Marquis informed the family, at breakfaft, that his affairs called him to Paris, and that they muft quit Champcery in two days. This news afflicted the children; but the Marquis gave them confolation, by affuring them, he was determined every year to remain fix months at Champcery.

Cæfar and his fifters could not leave Burgundy with dry eyes; and the grief of Auguftin was very great at leaving his father, his mother, and his little Charley. They fat off mournfully, but they became merrier on the road, and found all their ufual gaity and good-humour return by the time they came to Paris. After a few days of repofe, Madame de Clémire took her children to fee the Exhibition, at the Louvre, of the Paintings which are there fhewn, every other year, by the Artifts belonging to the Academy. The children could draw remarkably well for their age, had already acquired a love of the Arts, and the Sa-

loon

loon of the Louvre gave them great pleafure; fo
that they fpoke only of Pictures and Paintings the
reft of the day.

That lady, mamma, faid Caroline, who has
done thofe paintings which every body fo much
admires, is furely not young; for it is impoffible
in youth to have fuch fuperior talents.

How can you think fo, my dear? Have not you
feen her Portrait painted by herfelf?

Yes; but I thought that was a former work——
And can fhe be fo young and fo handfome as that
charming Picture reprefents her to be?

Had her's been common abilities, her youth,
her fex, her beauty, and excellent reputation,
would certainly not have permitted others to judge
of her works with fo much feverity.

I think fhe ought to infpire admiration indeed,
fince to all thefe advantages fhe adds that very
uncommon one of fuperior genius.

The Public are juft, and cannot be prevented
from praifing whatever pleafes, and whatever
ftrikes; therefore you have feen this lady's Pictures
fix the attention of all who entered the Saloon.

It is very glorious for a woman to gain an
honourable place among the greateft Mafters.

Yes: but it is very dangerous.

Men cannot be jealous of a woman.

They

They sometimes disdain not to do us that honour; and when they have once begun, their animosity knows no bounds. They imagine that they alone have a right to struggle for fame; they are willing enough to flatter us, and even to be led by us, but they disdain to wonder at us. To return to Madame le Brun; as I said just now, had not her abilities been above mediocrity, she would have received nothing but adoration, have heard nothing but flattery; but she undertook to paint History, and has not been surpassed by any one Academician. This to be sure is very strange! ——Very revolting!——Very——!

The Abbé informed me, mamma, that the Journalists have given an account of the Exhibition. They have, no doubt, praised exceedingly those of Madame le Brun.

Oh no; they had too much prudence, too much circumspection, to praise a woman who really had merit. Generous and compassionate as they are, their praises have been lavished upon the envious, whom they have consoled as much as in them lies. The public admire none but superior faculties, or useful labours; as for them, they protect the Weak, and praise the Poor in ability: and as mediocrity is the fate of the multitude, they, by this conduct, gain a multitude of friends, and have a just claim to the gratitude of

D 5 the

the envious and the detractors of Genius; an extensive and a dangerous class, whose hatred is as active as it is envenomed.

And so, mamma, the Journalists have not done justice to Madame le Brun?

One Journal only has judged her works with equity; all the others have spoken in a manner that has surprized every body, who is unacquainted with the invariable principles and profound politics of these writers. The enemies of Madame le Brun cannot deny that her success has been great; they only can affirm it is unmerited.

But what are their proofs?

They alledge, that Madame le Brun's manner is little.

How so, mamma? Her subjects are taken from the Iliad; her figures large as life.

Or else allegories of the most sublime and ingenious nature, such is what they call a littleness of manner: they add, that hitherto she has painted only women.

Would they then persuade us, that superior talents are not necessary to paint a beautiful woman?

Exactly so; but they have forgot, that Albanus painted none but Venus, the Loves and Graces (a);

they

(a) Albanus was born at Bologna. His second wife was a very beautiful woman, and became the model of all the

Divinities

they have forgot all the beautiful Virgins of Raphael, of Guido, of Carlo Maratti, &c. and thus it is that Envy reafons.

I obferve, mamma, faid Pulcheria, with great pleafure, that there are many women at prefent worthy to rank with great Painters ; four in France are admitted of the Academy, without mentioning feveral others, who have much greater abilities than certain Academicians.

In fact, we have feen fome very good-for-nothing Paintings in the Saloon; among others, thofe you would not ftop to look at ; I faw them as I paffed, and they feemed to me very indifferent : indeed, without any claim to a place in an Exhibition like this, they ought to have been equally profcribed by good tafte and morality.

But let us return to thofe females, who have diftinguifhed themfelves fo much in this brilliant career. Among Foreigners, there is one very much celebrated, who has likewife applied herfelf

Divinities in his Paintings. He had twelve children fo beautiful, that they not only ferved him to paint the charming Groups of Little Loves from, with which he enriched his fine compofitions, but were alfo the originals, after which Le Pouffin, Francis Flamand, and Algardi, (the latter was a Sculptor) ftudied the Graces of Infancy. Albanus died in 1660, aged 83. *Extraits des différens euvrages publiés fur la Vie des Peintres.* By M. M. P. D. L. F. Tom. I.

to the fublime. You have admired a multitude of Engravings done after her Pictures——I mean Angelica Kauffman.——I know not how the Journalists have treated her in the country where fhe lives, but her fuperior talents have been acknowledged by all Europe.

Since, mamma, you take fo much pleafure in collecting whatever is to the glory of women, perhaps, you know the names of all thofe who have acquired reputation in this art?

I can nearly remember them all.

Oh dear mamma, do tell us; we have heard already of Johanna Gazzoni (a); Elizabeth Cirani; Maria, the daughter of Tintoret (b); and of Rofalba (c).

(a) In Italy, and particularly at Rome, there are many of her Paintings in great eftimation.

(b) She died in 1590. There is a fine Painting by her in the Palais-Royal, of a Man fitting clothed in black, with his hand on an open book, lying on a table, where is a crucifix, an ink-ftand, a clock, and papers.

(c) Rofalba Carriera, was the Scholar of the Chevalier Diamantino, and furpaffed her Mafter. She acquired fuch great reputation, that all the Academies of Europe were eager to admit her. She was received a Member of the Academy at Paris in 1720; her Admiffion Picture was a Mufe in Crayons. She was paffionately fond of Mufic; played in a fup·rior ftyle on the Harpfichord, and travelled into France and Germany. Her merit procured her riches, and fhe died at Venice, in 1757, aged 85.

I will

I will give you a lift of the names of women moft celebrated for their Paintings (2). It would require a large volume to fpeak of them all; and it is the effect of prejudice that the number is not equal to that of the men who have been eminent Painters, which judges us incapable of works where genius is required. When they condefcend, which is very rare, to employ themfelves a little on our education, they wifh only to give us vague notions, confequently often falfe, fuperficial knowledge, and frivolous talents.

Does a Painter intend to inftruct his daughter in his art, he never conceives the project of making her a Painter of Hiftory, but will continually repeat fhe fhould pretend only to paint Portraits, Miniatures, or Flower-Pieces. Thus is fhe difcouraged, and thus is the fire of fancy ftifled: fhe paints Rofes; fhe was born, perhaps, to paint Heroes.

Thus likewife, a man of letters, whofe daughter gives proofs of wit, and a love of Poetry, may be induced to cultivate thefe happy difpofitions; but what will his firft care be? Why to rob his Scholar of that confidence which infpires fortitude, and that ambition which furmounts difficulties. He prefcribes bounds to her attempts, and commands her not to go beyond them. Like the
proud

proud Roman (*a*), who, taking advantage of his power and public opinion, impofed extravagant laws in fupport of prejudices; fo the Teacher traces a narrow circle round his young Pupil, over which fhe is forbid to ftep. Has fhe the genius of Corneille or Racine, fhe is conftantly told to write nothing but Novels, Paftorals, or Sonnets.

A celebrated Mufician brought me to hear his Niece, about two years fince, who played excellently on the Piano Forte. I admired particularly the manner in which fhe modulated, and learned, with extream furprize, fhe fcarcely knew the rules of Thorough Bafs. I afked why, with fuch propenfities, he had not taught her compofition?——Oh, I would not let her lofe her time about that, faid the Uncle; *What fervice can Compofition be of to a woman?*

All men reafon, refpecting us, like this impertinent Uncle; they are willing to allow we play on inftruments, we dance, and even we talk as well as they, becaufe thefe are facts that cannot be denied. There exifts another talent, however, equally common to women as to men; and this enchanting and fublime art necessarily demands lively and fine feelings, energy, enthufiafm, and

(*a*) Popilius. See Annales de la Vertu, Tom. **II.** Page 23.

all

all the great emotions of the mind, which, according to them, belong only to the men.

Ay, mamma, what is that?

The art of an Actress.

Oh true, mamma, there have been a great number of celebrated Actresses.

Had all the other arts, as well as this, been less the fruits of education and study, than the happy gifts of nature, there is no doubt but there would have existed a perfect equality between men and women.

Some days after this conversation, the children went to see the Luxembourg Gallery; and being questioned on their return by Madame de Clémire, they owned they had not remarked the Deluge, by Poussin (a). At your age, said their mamma, the

(a) Nicholas Poussin was born of a noble family, in 1594, at Andeli, a small town of Vexin-Normandy, and became one of the greatest Painters in the French School. He went to study at Rome, but the Cardinal de Richlieu invited him to Paris, where Louis XIII. gave him a pension, and the title of his First Painter; but the envy of inferior Artists obliged him to quit his native country, and return to Rome; though not till he had painted for the King's Cabinet a Ceiling, on which Time was represented, delivering Truth from the oppression of Envy. He died at Rome in 1665. We know no Scholar of his, except Guaspré, his Brother-in-Law, who took the name of Poussin.

pleasing,

pleafing, the dazzling, or the affecting only are remarked ; fubjects that infpire horror, pity, &c. catch the eye ; while the delicate and profound efcape notice : but I, by converfing with you, may inform you of what you at prefent could have but a very imperfect idea ; by which means I fhall infenfibly ftrengthen your judgments and form your tafte.

I remember to have feen the Painting you mention, mamma, but I own I found nothing in it very beautiful.

You have feen it rain often enough.

Certainly, mamma.

And have you ever, at fuch times, obferved the colour of the clouds attentively ; how the dufky atmofphere obfcures all objects, deftroys their brightnefs, fhades their tints, makes them, if diftant, difappear, or to be feen with difficulty ?

I cannot fay I have remarked all this.

Had you paid a proper attention to the effects of rain, you would have been amazed at the exactitude with which they have been painted by Pouffin ; but the greateft merit of this fublime Picture is in the compofition. · Forget that you have feen it, and tell me if you were going to paint the Univerfal Deluge, what idea do you fuppofe would firft offer itfelf to your imagination ?

That

That of reprefenting a multitude of men, ready to be buried beneath the waters.

It is true, that this idea naturally prefents itfelf; but in the execution, it would only have produced a vague and uninterefting fcene; it would have been beheld with as little emotion as battle pieces. Pouffin knew this; he felt, befides, that in painting this terrible cataftrophe, it was neceffary to chufe the moft ftriking point of time, which, no doubt, was at the moment when it was at the height.

He has, therefore, imagined five principal figures (a); but how interefting are thefe five people! They are not in the Ark, they are profcribed, muft fubmit to the fate of human kind, and perifh! Here you behold a mother, anxious but for her child; and, perifhing herfelf, thinks only how it may be faved! Here a hufband, ftretching out his arm to his wife; and there a man ready to voluntarily plunge himfelf from a boat into the deep——Doubtlefs to re-unite himfelf to whom he loves!

On one fide of this pathetic Picture, an object ftill more ftriking, more terrible, is feen; on the ridge of a rock, a Serpent appears; his attitude menacing, he raifes haughtily his proud head; you imagine you hear his horrible hiffing, and, fhud-

(a) Eleven in all, counting thofe whofe heads are juft feen above the water.

dering,

dering, recollect the tempting Spirit that made the firſt man fin, and that now applauds himſelf for being the Author of this new deſtruction.——— Hope, however, in ſome degree, ſoftens this ſcene of horrors, the eye is relieved by the happy Ark, which is ſeen afar off.

I now, mamma, comprehend the great merits of this Painting; I will hereafter examine the effects of rain with more attention, and ſhall be glad to return to the Luxembourg again, to behold the Deluge of Pouſſin.

We have ſeen another painting, the beauties of which we felt, *the birth of Louis XIII.* (*a*). We were made to obſerve the double expreſſion viſible in the countenance of Mary de Medicis, and we could not help admiring it.

Compoſition and expreſſion are the two eſſentials of painting, becauſe they ſpeak to the heart and underſtanding. A Painter not poſſeſſed of theſe, however great his knowledge of the other branches

(*a*) By Rubens. This illuſtrious Artiſt was born at Cologna, and acquired a great fortune; to the genius of a ſublime Painter, he added ſcientific knowledge; he knew ſeven languages, and wrote various works in Latin, ſome on the Rules of his Art, others on the coſtu-e of the Ancients: he was employed in ſeveral negociations, and died crowned with honour and wealth, at Antwerp, in 1640, aged 63. He had ſeveral ſcholars, and among others the celebrated Vandyke.

of his art, can never be thought a man of genius. To return to the picture of which you speak; that head of Mary de Medicis is really admirable. I never any where else saw this double expression of opposite passions on the same countenance, except in a piece of sculpture at Gènes. This is the *Chef-d'œuvre* of Puget, and represents the Martyrdom of Saint Sebastian. Here you behold on the visage of the Saint, the tortures of pain, and, at the same time, resignation and divine love.

It is necessary, mamma, that a great Painter should have acquired great knowledge.

Certainly; a Painter must indispensibly study Anatomy; he cannot thoroughly understand Perspective, without learning the elements of Geometry; he ought to have an intimate acquaintance with History and Mythology, ancient and modern: he should be a man of observation, and a Philosopher; and if he has not made the human heart his greatest study, he will never become sublime.

The requisites are so many, and so great, mamma, that I am not astonished we have so few fine Painters.

We do not seem at present to have any idea of what is possible for Genius and Industry to perform. The famous Raphael died at thirty-seven, yet he was a good Sculptor, an excellent Architect, and

and the greatest Painter that ever existed (a).
Michael Angelo likewise was superiorly great in
Sculpture, Architecture, and Painting (b). But
the excessive increase of luxury, by multiplying
frivolous amusements, drags us from retreat and
study, and deprives us of industry. Painters, in
our time, are not only ignorant of Sculpture and
Architecture, but I am afraid they read little ; for,
in general, they chuse none but common-place
subjects ; and, what is worse, they treat these subjects in a common-place manner.

But, mamma, how should it be otherwise, when
a subject has been so often used ?

(a) There is a Jonas by Raphael, at Rome, said to be
a master-piece in its kind, likewise several Palaces built
after his designs. He was born at Urbin, and died in
1520. His body, after having lain three days in the great
Hall of the Vatican, under his famous picture of the
Transfiguration, was carried to the Rotunda, preceded
by this same picture; the most glorious monument of
his labours and his genius, and which Leo X. made con-
ducive to the funeral pomp of this sublime Artist.

(b) I find in the life of Michael Angelo, that he was
the first Inventor of that species of modern Fortification,
by which he defended his native city of Florence, and
obliged the enemy to raise the siege. Among other
remains of sculpture by this Artist, the statue, at Rome,
of Moses holding the Book of the Law under his arm, is
particularly admired. He died, aged 90, in 1564.

To

To Genius, nothing is more eafy ; in painting efpecially : of which I will cite you two remarkable examples. I dare fay you have feen above a hundred *Roman Charities:* have you not?

Oh! that we certainly have.

There is not a collection of pictures, in which one Roman charity at leaft is not found. What think you of the one I am going to defcribe ?——— A young woman fuckles her father in prifon, her child lies weeping in her arms, and feems by its cries to demand a fubfiftence which nature deftined for it, while the mother beholds it with tendernefs and grief (*a*).

This is indeed a new effect, mamma, and yet the fame fubject.

The Painter has only added a fingle circumftance to produce this great effect.

But have you a right to invent circumftances in hiftorical facts ?

No doubt, if they are probable. Genius, however, finds other means, as in the fecond example I fhall cite. All Painters, who take the fubject of Judith and Holofernes, think they cannot do better than reprefent a woman of a mafculine figure, and a martial air, whofe menacing front announces her warlike genius. This, however,

(*a*) This painting is in the Spada Palace at Rome. The idea is beautiful, the execution indifferent.

was

was not Judith's character; she was a homicide only to save her country, and because she believed herself inspired by heaven. So saith the story. It is therefore very possible, that Judith had the natural mildness, modesty, and timidity of her sex; and that, carried away by the love of her country and divine inspiration, she committed an act which she could not otherwise have done. Enthusiasm has often produced events as extraordinary.

This is exactly what Paul Veronese has supposed in his divine picture; he has represented Judith beauteous, delicate, ingenuous, modest, timid, and with an angelic sweetness in her physiognomy. She holds in her fair hand the bloody head of Holofernes, and turns her eyes from the fearful object; her countenance does not express the horror of remorse, but the affections of pity; and while we look, we feel how much such an action must have cost her. It is impossible to behold this picture without great emotion. An Ethiopian woman holds a bag open; she considers, with ferocious curiosity, the head of Holofernes, and forms the most striking contrast to the mild and celestial Judith (a). This example may serve

to

(a) Paul Caliari Veronese was born at Verona in 1537. His most perfect picture is at Venice, in the Refectory of the Convent of St. George; the subject is the marriage

to convince you, that the resources of Genius are inexhaustible; and that force of imagination may be seen in the most common subjects.

Can you give us, mamma, said Caroline, any general rules, by which we may determine if a picture be good or bad?

To judge of paintings well, it is necessary, as I have before said, to observe the effects of nature, of Trees seen in perspective, of Rivers, Skies, Tempests, the rising and setting Sun, &c.

Then to become a Connoisseur, it is necessary to have lived in the country.

Yes, and to have travelled likewise; to have seen Mountains, Rocks, Precipices, natural Cascades, and all those great objects which Nature never unites in one spot: nay more, the Critic, like the Painter, ought to have a profound knowledge of the human heart; or how can he be certain of his judgment, when he says, " Such an " incident demands such a kind of expression."

In fact, it is impossible to be an excellent judge of paintings, without having seen a great number,

marriage of Cana. He died at Venice in 1588; his three sons were his disciples; the eldest, Charles, was particularly eminent, but he died at the age of 25. Verona gave birth likewise to another excellent Painter, Alexander Veronese, who called himself Turchi, or the Orbetto, and who died in 1670.

and

and having examined and compared them with the moſt careful attention. And after all, if the Amateur cannot draw and deſign, well or ill, there will be numberleſs beauties loſt to him.

How does it happen then, we have ſo many Connoiſſeurs ?

It is certain there never were ſo many collections formed : the Journaliſts aſſure us they are Connoiſſeurs, and, to prove they are, they make uſe of all the ſcientific terms adopted by certain Amateurs ; they ſay that an Artiſt has a *free hand*, that his outlines are *too hard* or *too ſoft*, that his colouring is *too warm* or *too cold*, with many others of a ſimilar kind.

Theſe expreſſions are very droll ; are they the terms of the art ?

I am willing to ſuppoſe ſo ; but it is certain, that a man much ſuperior to moſt of our Connoiſſeurs, has ſeldom employed them in an excellent treatiſe he has written on painting. This great Painter, admired at Rome, as much as in the reſt of Europe, has left a moſt uſeful and eſtimable work, which the ignorant as well as the Artiſt may read with pleaſure, and in which neither barbarous words nor ridiculous expreſſions are to be found (*a*).

Thoſe

(*a*) Anthony Raphael Mengs, born at Dreſden in 1728. The celebrated Winckleman has made the following eulogium on this great Artiſt, whom the world has lately loſt.

" An

Those who happily have new ideas, feek not new words to explain themfelves: they wifh to be well underftood, for they know that is the thing moft effential.

To return to the general rules you wifhed; admitting that the Amateur has acquired moft of the previous knowledge I have mentioned, his firft care fhould be to examine the clafs to which each fubject belongs; of which hiftory is the firft (a).

Let us then fuppofe the Connoifleur examining an hiftorical painting.

" An abftract of all the beauties, which ancient Artifts
" have difperfed among their figures, may be found in
" the immortal works of Raphael Mengs, firft Painter
" to the Courts of Spain and Poland; firft Artift of his
" age, and perhaps the firft of future ages. Like the
" Phœnix, it may be faid Raphael has rifen from his
" afhes, to teach the univerfe perfection in his Art, and
" attain it himfelf, as far as is poffible to man. It re-
" mained for Germany to produce a reftorer of Painting,
" to fhew the world a German Raphael, acknowledged
" fuch, and fo admired at Rome itfelf, the feat of the
" Arts." Hiftoire de l'Art, Tome I. page 312.----An
excellent tranflation in French, of the work of Mengs,
dedicated to Madame le Brun, cites the above eulogium.

(a) This clafs comprehends all great fubjects of Imagination, of Allegory and Mythology.

Give

Give me a fubject?

This propofition at firft embarraffed the children but, after a little reflection, they gave for fubject, Bias (*a*), purchafing the maidens of Meffina.———I am pleafed with the fubject, faid Madame de Clémire; it is interefting, and affords likewife the contraft of age, a diverfity of expreffion, and the fine coftûme of the Greeks. Do you form the compofition, and I will criticife : firft, where would you lay the fcene ?

On the fea-fhore, or in the houfe of Bias.

The houfe of a Philofopher ought to be fimple, without colonades or pilafters.

Let it be the fea-fhore then. The veffel of the Pirates is feen at a diftance; they have juft landed the young maidens, Bias purchafes them, fpeaks to the two Pirates, and gives them the money; mean time the young maidens affemble, form a beautiful group, and exprefs their joy.

Would it not be more interefting, were they to exprefs their gratitude?

Oh, yes ; fo it would.

The Pirates having received their money, are employed counting it in the back ground. Bias and the young maidens muft neceffarily be the

principal

(*a*) BIAS, one of the feven Sages. See Annales de la Virtue, Tome I. page 281.

principal figures. How would you reprefent Bias, and what expreffion ought he to have?

That of a venerable old man, with fatisfaction in his countenance.

And emotion, but with dignity; and without fuffering that expreffion to deprive him of the majeftic ferenity, which ought to be vifible in the phyfiognomy of a Sage. What action would you give the young maidens?

They may embrace him, he being old and virtuous.

But he is a man, and young maidens are always modeft, timid, and with lively feelings; and fhould fo be reprefented, if you wifh them to be affecting. What age would you give them?

They fhould be fixteen or feventeen.

That would have a monotonous effect; I fhould make one of them a girl of eight years old, another of eighteen, a third of twelve, and the reft of fourteen or fifteen. The youngeft, with all the innocence of her age, fhould run into the arms of the Philofopher to embrace him; the eldeft, as her who is moft likely to fpeak and feel the benefit they had received with the greateft energy, fhould kneel to him; fhe likewife might clafp her young fifter of twelve to her bofom, and prefent her to the Sage; her countenance fhould exprefs her gratitude, and her companions, who are arranged

E 2 ranged

ranged behind her, would form an affecting group.

Why should they not come forward?

Timidity will not permit them; at their age, they cannot vanquish this fenfation, even when very ill timed.

I now comprehend the whole; I fee our Picture, and think it excellent.

Yes; but there are two characters, the Pirates, who take no part in the principal action, who do not attend to it, and this is a defect in the compofition.

Let us fuppofe them not in the picture.

Nay, but they are neceffary to the ftory; without them, you could not divine what the fubject might be.

Why may not the Pirates attend to the principal Group, while counting their money?

Nothing fhould affect Pirates who are counting money.

Let us fuppofe the money divided, and take the moment when one of them is putting up his purfe; the eye of the other being attracted, he jogs his companion, to make him obferve what is going forward. What expreffion would you give him who is looking?

An expreffion of mere curiofity.

Very

Very well; I think our Picture is now tolerably well composed (*a*).

Let us compose a Picture every day, mamma; we will each, by turns, give a subject. Will not that be charming?

I am willing, provided you can now tell me, and in few words, what is requisite to be observed, in general, in order to judge of the merit of a Painting, relative to it's composition.

That is very easy; you have just taught us.

Well, let me hear.

It is first necessary, that the subject should be easily known by all those who have read the story it represents; it should next be observed, whether the point of time be well chosen, and, also, the place; if the characters have such attitudes and such expression as their age and circumstance require; and, lastly, if the costûme be well observed.

(*a*) In Pictures where the Figures are not mere Accessaries, as in Landscapes, it is necessary they should fill up the greatest part of the canvas, especially when the subject affords many Figures. There is another important rule to be observed in composition, which is, that the Figures in the Back-Ground ought not to have equal strength of expression with those in the Fore-Ground, but there should be a gradation of passion consonant to the Perspective.

You

You have perfectly underftood all I have faid.

And may we compofe an Hiftorical picture every evening, like as we have done to-day?

Yes, I give you my word; and when, next fpring, we fhall be at Champcery, we will chufe other fubjects, of the ruftic kind, fuch as Teniers (*a*) and Gerard-Dow (*b*) ufed to paint.

We fhall have the very models before us.

So Painters ought to have. Underftand, however, this ftyle of painting is much inferior to the other. Woe be to him that prefers the reprefentation

tion

(*a*) David Teniers the Elder, was born at Antwerp, in 1582. He was the Scholar of Rubens, and painted only Laboratories, Smoking Rooms, Dutch Fairs, and fimilar fubjects. His fon David Teniers was yet more eminent in the fame ftyle. Abraham his brother was inferior to both.

(*b*) Gerard-Dow was born at Leyden, in 1613, and was the Pupil of Rembrant. He died in 1680. His beft Difciples were Skalken and Miers, and his fineft Pictures the Quack Doctor, and the Dropfical Woman: the firft is in the Duffeldorp Gallery, and the fecond at Turin, in the King of Sardinia's Collection. It reprefents a Dropfical Woman, of an interefting countenence, fitting in an arm-chair, while an Empiric, in a long fatin robe, examines a phial, which contains a liquid; the woman's daughter is kneeling before her, looking with great expreffion of pity in her face, and weeping.

tion of an Ale-house, or a woman felling Carrots and Cabbages, to the works of Raphael and Correggio (a).

The Comic Style cannot exift in Painting, becaufe no Pantomime can be interefting without a Denoument, and efpecially without action; let him imagine every thing that is ridiculous, every thing the moft grotefque, he will never have the trifling merit of a Buffoon; he will never make any body burft into a laugh; he can only be low and grofs, cannot be pleafant. Painting has the power to foften, to pleafe; can prefent gentle and agreeable images; can infpire pity, terror, and admiration; but never real mirth. I often hear of the perfect truth of the Flemifh Paintings, but I regard not truth in Books or Pictures, except as it inftructs or affects me. I have no pleafure in looking at an old ugly Cook-Maid weeping over Onions; fome would be in raptures

(a) Antonio Allegri Corregio, was born at Corregio, in Modena, and is confidered as the Founder of the Lombardian School. He particularly attached himfelf to Grace, and no Painter has ever excelled him in the elegant. After confidering a Picture of Raphael's with great attention, he is faid to have exclaimed, *Anche io fon pittore* : And I too am a Painter." Corregio was a Mathematician alfo, and an Architect. He died in 1534, aged 40.

at

at beholding fuch a figure, but it fhould never find a place in my Cabinet. I fhall always be capricious enough to think a handfome fhepherdefs a more agreeable object; and I fhould ftill prefer to her a Nymph or a Goddefs, becaufe they prefent a more perfect model of Beauty.

If a Painting has not the merit of an ingenious or interefting compofition; if it only reprefents one or two inactive figures, they ought at leaft to be well imagined, and fuch as are worthy to fix the attention; like as, a venerable old Man, or a perfectly beautiful Woman. What pleafure can the exact imitation of a thing produce, which is not in its own nature deferving of notice? It requires no more genius to paint a Fifh-woman than a Flower-vafe; and certainly the laft ought to have the preference, fince it is the moft agreeable (*a*).

Permit me, mamma, faid Pulcheria, to afk you another queftion; I wifh to know particularly, in what the merit of an Allegory confifts?

An Allegory ought to be evident, that is to fay, eafy to underftand at firft fight; it ought to contain fome juft idea, or fome moral thought;

for

(*a*) *The Reader will form his own judgment of thefe opinions on the Comic in Painting; it feems evident, however, that Madame de Genlis has never feen the Works of Hogarth, or at leaft never ftudied them.* T.

for example, *Innocence throwing herself into the arms of Justice*; or *Peace conducting Plenty* (a). These Allegories at once afford delightful images, and just and moral ideas. *Time unveiling Truth*, is an old Allegory, but must always please, because of it's propriety. It has, however, one defect, which is, that the Figure of Truth has not Attributes sufficiently marking to be known without hesitation. Some affert that Truth should be represented as a majestic Woman, simply clothed; others pretend she should be naked; for which reason, the personification of this Virtue becomes confused.

But has not the Allegory you have just mentioned, the same defect? Has Innocence any known Attributes?

They often give it such as can only serve to lead the mind aftray; as a Dove, for instance, which is one of the Infignia of Venus; but Innocence needs no attributes, under the hands of an Artist of genius; it will then be sufficiently eafy to divine by the neceffary expreffion. Truth has no fuch advantage: she is painted beautiful, noble, and cold, but fo may a Nymph or Goddefs be; therefore she is neither characterifed by her Attributes nor her Phyfiognomy; but the expreffion of innocence belongs only to Innocence;

E 5   she

(a) Both by Madame le Brun.

she cannot be confounded with Nymphs, Graces, and Goddesses, who are neither so youthful nor so affecting as herself; her Attributes are on her face, in her eyes; an interesting mixture of timidity, modesty, and gentleness, embellishes and speaks who she is. Pure and celestial Figure, the extent of whose charms the delicate pencil of a woman alone can trace !

Hence you may learn, it requires much less genius to paint Allegorical Figures with material Attributes, than to represent those who can only be characterised by the expression of the countenance; for it is much easier to paint a cornucopia, or a pair of wings, than an expressive face. Rubens has represented Ignorance in the Luxembourg Gallery: the Figure has no Attributes, yet is as soon and generally known as Time or Discord. None but a superior Artist could have given this degree of truth to an affection of the mind.

Consequently there are no Passions, Vices, or Virtues, which may not be painted allegorically?

Oh yes, but there are, and many, which a Painter can convey no idea of, or at least none but vague and obscure ones. All those who want both Attributes and characteristic expression, ought, for this reason, to be rejected in general. Benevolence, for instance, is a Virtue without Attributes

or

or Expreffion, peculiar to itfelf, and may be confounded with Pity.

It feems to me, mamma, Painters ought to read Poetry as well as Hiftory, and then they need not want Allegories.

You are very right; but they generally read little, except Tranflations from Homer and Taffo; whereas Milton and others might furnifh them with fubjects lefs hacknied, and equally noble; they might find, alfo, in our French Poets, a multitude of charming images and ideas. Thus, if an Artift wifhed to depict Hygeia, the Goddefs of Health, *Greffet* will furnifh him with an excellent Group of Figures. I will read you his defcription of her, and after the firft fix lines, do you imagine to yourfelves I am defcribing Beings, which muft each in order be placed upon the Canvas.

As Hebe fwift, as Venus fair,
Youthful, rofy, light as air,
She comes, difperfing Ills and Glooms,
And Courage glows, and Beauty blooms;
Fits, Faintings, Languors, tottering fly
The vivid glances of her Eye.
So Cupid, Bacchus', Morpheus are
Attendants on her jocund Car;
While fhe, with Vine and Myrtle crown'd,
Beholds extended on the ground

The

The God of Epidaurus (*a*) thrown,
His pow'r contemn'd, his art unknown:

True, mamma, replied Pulcheria, a charming
Picture, indeed, might be formed from this defcription.

I have always forgot, faid Cæfar, to afk my
mamma a thing which I juft now recollect. A
few days fince we faw a piece of Sculpture, reprefenting a woman at the bath, attended by a Negrefs. The figure bathing is of white marble, but
the Negrefs is in bronze.

I know this performance, it is charming, and
the name of the Artift who is the author of
it, is a fufficient eulogium. There is a reafon
why the Negrefs is in bronze. She holds a vafe
of water, and it was neceffary to have leaden
pipes pafs through the Statue, in order to fend
the water into the Vafe: this could not have been
executed had the ftatue been of marble; otherwife,
the Artift would, certainly, never have jumbled
marble and bronze in the fame compofition; he
has too much tafte not to feel the effect could not
be happy.

There is a ftatue of Saint Staniflaus at Rome
in his religious habit. The robe is of black marble, and the figure of white; which medley is
more fhocking than the one we have juft mentioned.

(*a*) The Statue of Æfculapius.

tioned, and muſt deſtroy, not add to, the de-
luſion. If, while examining ſculpture, the mind is
not wholly occupied by the idea of form, if any
acceſſary introduces that of colour, if the drapery
is repreſented ſhort, and with natural ſhades, the
Spectator would immediately require the carnation
of the face, and, wanting it, would only behold a
Doll, ridiculouſly clothed.

I can eaſily ſuppoſe that, mamma; but why then
is this very ſame thing admired in ſeal engraving?

Becauſe heads cut in a ſeal or a ring, can never,
any way, produce the ſlighteſt degree of illuſion.
The things wiſhed there, are elegance and purity
of deſign; and it is reaſonable to praiſe the Artiſt
who knows how to bring forth the beauties of the
ſtone, by taking an ingenious advantage of the
natural colours it poſſeſſes.

I am glad, mamma, of this explanation, for I
confeſs it was this very mixture, white and black,
that pleaſed me; I thought it fine, becauſe I had
never ſeen the like before.

Hereafter you will know, that it is not ſufficient
for an idea to be new, it muſt alſo be natural. If
an invention is neither uſeful nor agreeable, it is
not meritorious but capricious; and reſembles the
whims of the Sicilian Prince, of whom I ſpoke to
you the other day: it is productive of extravagance,
it brings forth Monſters (3).

They

They now came to inform Madame de Clémire her carriage was ready, and she took the children to the Comedy. As they returned they conversed on the play; and Cæsar was desirous his mamma should give him some general precepts, by which he might judge of dramatic works.——You are too young at present, said Madame de Clémire, to be properly informed on that subject; but I have the plan of a work, which I shall surely execute for the benefit of my children: it will be entitled *Cours de Litérature, a l'Usage des jeunnes personnes*. (A course of Literature for the use of young people.) This you shall read when you are sixteen or seventeen, and, with the addition of that most estimable work, called, *La Poetique*, by Marmontel, I have no doubt but you will have an enlarged knowledge of such things, and a good taste.

How many volumes will it make, mamma?

Three at most.

And will it be amusing?

I certainly shall neglect nothing that may give pleasure and variety, as much as possible; for I am well convinced, youth cannot be instructed by what is tiresome and dull. It will be my endeavour to draw my principles from nature, to convey clear and precise ideas, and to give you a general knowledge of French, English, Italian, and Spanish literature.

By

By this time the carriage entered the Court, they arrived, and fat down to fupper with laffitude ; all complained of the head-ache, and Cæfar and his fifters found, they no longer poffeffed the keen appetites and chearful fpirits the air of Champeery gave. They gaped at each other, they lolled in their chairs, they could not eat; and they all agreed, they fhould be forry to go every evening and be fhut up three hours in a box at the Play-houfe. The pleafures of walking, reading, and converfing, they all owned were preferable to any thing the Theatre could afford.

Not but that they walked at Paris, but then it was in the gardens of the Tuilleries, the Palais-Royal, or the Elyfian Fields, where decorum muft be obferved, and where they only regretted the Woods, the Meadows, and the charming liberty of the fields of Burgundy. Cæfar feverely criti-cifed every thing he faw. What a duft! cried he. What a crowd! And what do thefe people come here for, to ftare and run in each others way, and hinder me from running and climbing up the trees?

And thefe large bafins of ftagnant water, faid Caroline, are they equal to our pond at Faulin, where we have angled and caught fo many fifh? And then, inftead of our blackberries and filbert-nuts, to fee nothing but trimmed evergreens, ftone

walls,

walls, or iron-gates! No plants, no flowers. Oh what dull gardens! How can people shut themselves up here, for ever, when they might live in the country!

Madame de Clémire heard these murmurs; but did not disapprove them, because they were well founded; but she took the children to the King's garden, which they found more instructive, and almost as pleasant as the Woods of Champcery. The study of Botany and natural History, rendered these walks so agreeable, that they would think of no other during the rest of Autumn.

Winter came, and with it new repinings. They recollected, sighing, the frozen ponds of the country, their slides, their snow-balls, and their evening stories; in fine, all the pleasures of which they were deprived. The balls of Paris were but a poor recompense; they afforded but little amusement, and they always returned fatigued and disappointed. In the month of January Caroline had so bad a cold, that she was obliged to have a separate chamber, because she disturbed her sister so much in the night, by which means Pulcheria was left alone.

In about five or six days time Madame de Clémire learnt, that Pulcheria, notwithstanding the excessive cold, sat without a fire in her room, and that she would not let them make one ever

since

since her Sister's indisposition. Surprised at this
fancy, Madame de Clémire questioned the servants. The *Frotteur*, whose business it was to
bring the wood, declared, that Mademoiselle Pulcheria had desired him to put her three faggots,
every morning, at the bottom of the closet, in the
anti-chamber. For my part, madam, said the
Frotteur, I asked no questions, though I thought
it odd, because I thought it was my lady's pleasure.

The Governante was solely employed in the
care of Caroline, and had not been in Pulcheria's
chamber, who was now waited on by a young
girl they had brought out of Burgundy; and
who, being interrogated in her turn, said, that
Mademoiselle Pulcheria had told her she did not
chuse fire, but that she would accustom herself to
bear the cold.

After getting all the intelligence she could, Madame de Clémire went up to Pulcheria's apartment:
the bottom of the closet was first visited, but not a
single faggot was there to be found. She then entered
her daughter's chamber. It was about ten o'clock
in the morning, and Pulcheria was walking, at a
good pace, up and down the room, to keep herself
warm, while she was repeating her task. Gertrude, her country maid, was sitting in a corner
knitting. As soon as Pulcheria saw her mamma
she blushed.——How now, said Madame de Clémire,

mire, how does it happen child, that you are without fire?

Oh, I can keep myself warm, mamma.

Madame de Clémire sat down, and sent away Gertrude, then taking Pulcheria by the hand, said, you will, now, I am sure, my dear, speak to me as to a friend.

I will tell you every thing, my dear mamma; but perhaps you have already guessed?

I have some confused suspicions.

You shall know all. About seven or eight days since, I heard my Governante telling how a poor woman, who lives in our street, had been to ask alms; my Governante gave her something, and went once afterwards to carry her bread. My Governante told me, that this poor woman desired nothing so much as to work for her living, but she could find nothing to do; and what is still more to be pitied, she had no firing. My Governante said she would furnish her with work, and I thought, if I could send her firing, she, then, would want nothing. I would not tell you of it, mamma, because I had already formed my project; I knew that my Sister was going to sleep in another chamber, and I said to myself, here is a fine opportunity of doing, like Sidonia, a good action in private. I will not even speak of it to mamma; for since time discovers all things, she will know

it

it foon or late; but it does not become me to be vain of it, and when known it will give the greater pleafure; in the mean while the poor woman will be happy, and God will behold the action. I then determined to pafs the morning without fire. by which means I fhould fave three faggots; and I defired the *Frotteur* to lay them at the bottom of the clofet, which he always did in the evening, to fave his labour the next morning. I was obliged to make a confidant of Jeanneton the chamber-maid, who at firft made fome objections; till I affured her, inftead of making you angry, mamma, it would give you great pleafure: fhe declared, however, that if you queftioned her fhe fhould tell the truth, but if you did not, fhe promifed me to be filent.

And did fhe undertake to carry the wood to the poor woman?

Yes, mamma, every morning.

But how could fhe pafs the outer gate, thus loaded, and regularly carrying three faggots?

Dear! I do not know; I never thought of that; the porter might well be furprized; and yet he cannot have afked her any queftions, fince fhe never faid any thing to me.

There is fomething at the bottom of this that we are ignorant of; but tell me, have you fuffered much from the cold?

A little,

A little, the two firſt days; but I remembered, that the poor woman and her little ones would warm themſelves, for ſhe has ſix ſmall children and a ſick huſband; but Jeanneton tells me, they are much better off now.

How ſo, with three faggots, only?

Yes. Jeanneton ſays they are quite enlivened, quite different people. To be ſure I ſent them, beſide the faggots, two boxes of candied orange-peel, for the children, that my papa brought me from Fontainebleau. That is not all: the day before yeſterday, I do not know how it happened, but my papa aſked me, if I ſhould not be glad to have ſome money to buy me play-things. At firſt I anſwered no; but I afterwards recollected the poor woman, and bluſhed. Papa kiſſed me, and gave me a guinea; after which, he enumerated how many things a guinea would buy; and I muſt own, I had a great deſire to lay out a crown of it in purchaſing pincuſhions; and yet this made me melancholy. I got my guinea changed, put a crown in my pocket, and giving the reſt to Jeanne-ton, bade her carry it to the poor woman, and added, that the next day I ſhould ſend her to buy me ſome pincuſhions. She left the room; I took my crown out of my pocket, and looked at it with uneaſineſs; for as I at firſt had intended to give the whole guinea to the poor woman, it

ſeemed

feemed to me, that I kept fomething which was not my own: away I ran to the ftair-head, to call back Jeanneton, but fhe was gone, and I faw her no more till the next morning. I waked be-times, and began to think on the pin-cufhions and the poor woman.——I was a good deal em-barraffed, but recollecting, at laft, this was the firft guinea I ever had in my life, I faid to my-felf, I muft employ it all in a good action: this thought determined me; Jeanneton arrived, and I fent her with the three faggots and the crown-piece.

Juft as Pulcheria had ended this recital a foot-man entered, and gave a note to Madame de Clémire, who, looking at the direction, faid to Pulcheria, it is addreffed to you, my dear; it is, no doubt, an invitation to a ball. So faying, fhe opened the note, and to the great aftonifhment of Pulcheria read as follows:

" Mademoifelle,

" Come and receive the recompenfe of your
" bounty to us; come and fee from what mifery
" you have relieved us; nothing is now wanting
" to our felicity, but to have her, to whom we are
" indebted for it, a witnefs of it. We cannot
" better prove our gratitude to our young, our
" dear Benefactrefs, than to fhew her the family
" fhe has rendered fo perfectly happy."

Dear

Dear mamma, cried Pulcheria, do, my good mamma, be kind enough to take me to fee thefe good people.

Certainly, my dear, replied Madame de Clémire; we will go directly, I will order the carriage. Come, come, my dear girl.

Madame de Clémire took Pulcheria by the hand, and away they went. At the bottom of the ftaircafe they met the Marquis. Where are you going? faid he; if you are going abroad, I am juft returned, and my carriage is ready.

We are: come, go with us, my dear.

Willingly, replied the Marquis. And, without afking farther queftions, gave the Marchionefs his arm.

Pulcheria followed with inexpreffible emotion. They entered their carriage, it departed, and, in about five minutes, ftopt. They alighted, croffed a little yard, the Marquis opened the door, and they found themfelves in a large chamber. In the midft of it they faw a Sadler at work, while a woman, fitting at a table, with fix little girls at her fide, the biggeft of whom was only ten years old, was bufy at her needle-work. The moment the Marquis de Clémire appeared, the whole family rofe; come hither, Madame le Blanc, faid the Marquis, this is Pulcheria.

Inftantly

Inftantly the wife, the hufband, the children, all flew to Pulcheria. Oh! my dear young lady, replied the woman, is it you? What at your age! And fo delicate too! Could you pafs thefe wintry days without fire, to fend us your wood ——Your money——Nay your very fweetmeats, every thing you had to give?——But behold! look how happy we are!—— My hufband is recovered, our debts are paid, our children are clothed, we are made capable of getting our living, we want for nothing, and you alone were the firft author of all our happinefs; for, had it not been for your goodnefs, your dear papa would never have known us.

Ah! papa, then Jeanneton has told you all.

From the very firft day, replied the Marquis; nay, I have more than once carried the faggots in my coach to Madame le Blanc; but I exprefsly forbad Jeanneton to fpeak of it to your mamma, or give you any hints that I was in the fecret; I wifhed to agreeably furprize you both.

After this explanation, the Marquis was tenderly kiffed by his wife and daughter; and they converfed for about half an hour with the good people, then rofe to take their leave. Juft at this moment the children ran to fetch a little box, and the eldeft prefenting it to Pulcheria, prayed her to accept it, faying, it is our own work; my mother,

.my

my filters, and myfelf, all have been bufy at it; and, I affure you, mademoifelle, with a right good-will.

Pulcheria opened the box, and found it full of the prettieft pincufhions fhe had ever feen. Pulcheria blufhed, then turning towards her father, faid, indeed, papa, I thought no more about them——but now with what pleafure do I receive them! fince they are the work of this good woman and charming little girls.

Pulcheria's heart was full; fhe kiffed the children, and the tears again came in her eyes, when, as fhe was going, fhe heard the benedictions of the whole family.——Oh my poor fifter, replied Pulcheria, as fhe got into the carriage, how forry I am her cold has prevented her from partaking the fatisfaction I now feel.——Permit me, mamma, continued fhe, fince I am accuftomed to do without fire, to give you my wood for the poor every winter.

No, replied Madame de Clémire, I muft not let you undertake to perform what at length muft become too painful; you know I have already told you, that thofe refolutions which demand a certain degree of perfeverance, are not for an age like your's; but, if you wifh every winter to renew the action you have juft done, that is to fay, to remain

eight

eight days without firing, and give it to some poor
family, you shall have my leave with all my heart.

Oh yes, yes, mamma, I will certainly do so.
——A thought has just struck me——Cannot I
also do without wine at my dinner, for a certain
space of time, and give it to the same poor family?

You drink so little, that you would be a con-
siderable time in saving half a bottle only.

But when I shall be grown up, mamma, how
much shall I then drink in eight days?

Four bottles at the very most.

If it were but three, it would be very acceptable
to a sick person.

Certainly, three bottles of good wine might be
a precious and salutary present; and if we were to
go eight days every month without wine, our
health would be the better for it, and our very
pleasure in tasting it increased.

By such means, then, one may give alms, and
yet not be rich.

Without any extra expence, it is possible, in
the course of the year, to succour a great number of people, if we would only, occasionally, deprive ourselves of superfluities. Let me observe,
too, that a momentary privation is productive of
certain pleasure; for example, when you have
remained all the morning without a fire, and
come down into the drawing-room, at one

o'clock, do you not experience a pleasure which you would not have felt, if you had been sitting over a fire in your own room?

Oh yes, mamma, I warm myself with extream satisfaction; the very sight of the fire, somehow, makes me quite happy.

Hence then you find, that pleasure is every way at accord with benevolence; for the sweet delight of doing a good action is, as you have just experienced, the greatest of all possible pleasures.

How does it happen, mamma, that there are people who do not know, nor feel this?

A trifling vanity, and a silly love of shew, corrupt many hearts; yet, even here, where luxuries so often stifle virtue, we may find examples that do honour to the age; the anonymous alms, only, sent to the different Curates of Paris, are immense. A multitude of prisoners every month, composed of unfortunate tradesmen, owe liberty, and the pleasure of again seeing their children, to persons unknown. Benevolence has founded prizes in all the Academies; it has formed, in Paris and its environs, useful and respectable establishments. How natural then is virtue to the heart of man, since it predominates in a place where it is combated by so many factitious and puerile passions, which a contemptible and foolish vanity produces.

Here

Here this conversation ended; for Madame de Clémire, desirous of knowing how Caroline did, rose, took Pulcheria with her, and went to her chamber. Caroline's cough was something worse; she had eaten a little cake of dried cherries, not knowing that what was very healthy, in general, might be bad for her cold. Madame de Clémire took this occasion of repeating to her children, how necessary it was to understand the properties of our usual food; since this knowledge, added to temperance, will prevent a thousand inconveniencies, and many very dreadful diseases.

As soon as Caroline was recovered, her mamma took her children to a new Opera, with which they were all highly delighted. The next day, their studies being all over, the children came and sat with their mamma till supper-time; there was company, and the conversation turned on the Opera. What madam, said a little man, who spoke excessively loud to the Marchioness, is it possible, madam, you can be pleased with the music?

Exceedingly.

But you have been a Gluckist these two years.

And as I have neither forgotten nor ceased to love good music, I am so still.

If so, you ought not to be pleased with the new Opera.

F 2

No,

No, Sir! why not?

Because it is impossible to love two styles of composition so absolutely opposite.

I believe it is as impossible to love the good and the bad, as it is to esteem a fool and a man of understanding; but I believe, and I feel, I can take pleasure in different styles of composition, though, Sir, as you say, absolutely opposite; for which reason, I love Corneille, Racine, Gluck, and Piccini.

But do you conceive the consequence of this impartiality? Your suffrage will please neither the Partisans of Gluck nor of Piccini.

May be so, but I shall have the double pleasure of admiring them both; and as to glory, I prefer that of being equitable, to that of obtaining the praises of either of their Partisans.

But, speak truly, is it possible you can love *Orphée*, *Iphigénie*, *Alceste*, *Armide?* ——— The music of Vandals! ——— A monstrous and detestable creation!

A visitor arrived, Madame de Clémire changed the conversation, and the little man, finding nobody to dispute with, grew dull, and retired in a very ill-humour.

As soon as the children were alone with Madame de Clémire, dear mamma, said Caroline, how terribly you vexed the gentleman who went away so abruptly. He who had so great an aversion to Gluck.

M. de

M. de Volny you mean?——Did you think his behaviour polite, rational, moderate?

Oh dear no, and he fpoke in fuch a manner.

He was angry, yet you faid nothing to offend him.

No, but fo is ever the fpirit of party. Remember therefore, no perfon can be uniformly well-behaved and reafonable, without a total impartiality.

What did he mean, mamma, by Vandals, and a deteftable creation? I did not underftand him.

'He did not underftand himfelf; he has no knowledge of mufic.

No! and yet decide with fo much confidence.

It is the fafhion at prefent; thofe who do not know how to beat time to an air, who cannot diftinguifh perfect harmony from a difcord, and who, while they liften, know not when one movement ends and another begins, argue, learnedly, on compofition, and even write books to prove that Piccini has no genius, or that Gluck is a Barbarian.

Can one be a Connoiffeur in mufic, mamma, without a knowledge of the fcience?

No; that is abfolutely impoffible. We have already allowed, that, with the beft natural tafte poffible, after long ftudy, after travelling and obferving with attention the varieties of nature, and all the collections of pictures in Europe, an

F 3 'Amateur,

Amateur, if he cannot paint himfelf, never can diftinguifh all the beauties of a picture vifible to a good Painter: yet painting is a real imitation of nature; it reprefents material objects as they are hourly feen, and many parts of it muft equally pleafe the ignorant and the learned; the nicer touches of art efcape the firft, but they cannot help being pleafed with an imitation that looks like nature itfelf.

It is not the fame with mufic; the compofer of an Opera, no doubt, muft find, in nature, that kind of declamation which his Poem requires; but this fpecies of imitation is too abftracted, to be as generally felt as that of painting. Befides, mufic may have expreffion and yet not be good: as, for example, if certain rules of compofition are not obferved, which, however, none but a Mufician will properly feel the defect of. I own that, in general, it is my opinion, fenfibility and good tafte may, without a knowledge of mufic, diftinguifh the merits of certain paffages, where the expreffion is very happy; may feel the difference of ftyle, and determine if the melody be agreeable, or common and infipid; but it is impoffible they can hear the beauties or defects of complicated harmony; they abfolutely do not hear them, they are deaf to the effects of an accompanyment. I fuftain (and the proof is eafy) that a perfon who does not

underftand

understand music, that is to say, who cannot de-
cypher it with facility, and whose youth has not
been past in composing it, will never thoroughly
know it: let another modulate, and give a mixture of good and false concord; and let this be a
person of reputation, and you shall see one of these
Connoisseurs, who declaim so emphatically on
barbarous music, motives, and intentions, listen, with
delight, to discords and unconnected resolutions of
harmony, which would make a Musician shudder,
and bestow the most pompous praises while he
listens. And what do people gain, who wish to
seem learned in things they know nothing about?
They impose on nobody, they talk nonsensically,
they judge without taste, they are accused of pedantry
by the ignorant, of folly by the well-informed, and
they are tiresome and disagreeable to both (4).

Some days after this conversation, Cæsar one
morning entered the chamber of the Marquis,
holding a newspaper in his hand, and said, I am
come, papa, to ask you a question concerning a
thing which to me appears very extraordinary;
look, here is *the Journal de Paris*, the Abbé gives
it me to read every time he finds a benevolent
action recounted in it.

He must give it you very often then, for scarce
a day passes in which you do not see the word
BENEVOLENCE, printed in large characters.

F 4   Yes,

Yes, papa, but this is what I am vexed at.

How so?

Because such a title bespeaks some great action, and in this Journal I am almost continually disappointed.—— Look, papa, what follows after the word Benevolence.

Yes, I see——It is a long story.

It takes up half the paper——Shall I tell it you, papa?

If you please.

A poor woman had placed her fire-pot under her clothes, and fell asleep. Somebody came in and found her burning; her petticoats were all in a flame, she had no longer the human form. The horse soldiers that guard the streets, arrived, and both they and the spectators were affected; the soldiers assisted the dying woman; a Surgeon asked for a little oil and some wine for her, and one of the soldiers went and got it; the Surgeon applied it to the poor patient, who was afterwards sent to the hospital, whither the soldiers conducted her.

Well, but relate the act of Benevolence.

I have, papa, it was the oil that the soldier went to seek.

That is not possible, Cæsar.

Nay, papa, there is the paper, read (a).

It

(a) *Journal de Paris*, No. 340, *samedi* 6 *Decembre*, 1783.

It is very true, you have omitted nothing——this must be seen to be believed.

As they must have been inhumanly barbarous not to have assisted that poor wretched woman, I am quite shocked to see them praise, with such emphasis, so natural an act; and dignify men with the title of benevolent, for merely fulfilling indispensible duties.

Your remark is just; he who thinks himself heroic for doing his duty, will never get any farther, will never become virtuous : and, if every body agreed to think that benevolence, which is the mere office of humanity, benevolence would not long be seen upon earth.

Madame de Clémire and her daughters now came in; they breakfasted, and afterwards went abroad to visit cabinets of natural History, and collections of Paintings, which recreation Madame de Clémire procured her children twice a week. To give variety to these instructive amusements, they sometimes went to see manufactories, or works of architecture.

My children, said Madame de Clémire, if you wish to inhabit cities, to be happy in them, and not become a prey to lassitude, never give yourselves up to idle dissipation, which can neither satisfy the heart, nor occupy the mind ; never debase your taste by a frivolous and contemptible
love

love of shew; preserve carefully in your bosoms that active and tender compassion you owe the unfortunate; remember where luxury is most prevalent, there is misery most powerful; and recollect how little, often, may snatch Wretchedness from disease and death. You have some idea of the pure happiness which awaits you in the habitation of Want; search ardently, stretch out the hand of charity, and enjoy the glory and the delight of offering, to the eyes of Poverty, the merciful and sublime image of the Creator; of making the sweet tears of Gratitude, and the passionate transports of unexpected Joy, succeed the bitter cries of Despair.

Finally, my children, in these places of resort for genius and emulation, where in a thousand varied forms they daily present their labours, love the fine arts, encourage ingenuity and industry, and cultivate your minds, and extend your knowledge, in order to enjoy a number of rational pleasures, the value of which is unknown to ignorance. Yet let not even these instructive occupations, and these varied amusements, make you insensible to the sweet delights of a country life. Oh! may the remembrance of the Tales of the Castle never be effaced from your hearts; and may you never forget the charms, the innocence,

the

the variety, the true pleasures which simple Nature ever affords !

Madame de Clémire, at one of their evening converfations, had told her children she should write fome moral tales for their inftructions. As they grew up, and might venture to read with the affiftance of a Commentator, she gave them the three following Tales; faying, you may read, hereafter, many ftories infinitely more agreeable than mine, perhaps; but you will find, in thefe, morality and truth, at leaft ; and, if they pleafe you, I have three others which you fhall, one day, have to read.

THE

THE

TWO REPUTATIONS.

A MORAL TALE.

LUZINCOURT, satisfied with a moderate fortune, and an obscure, but peaceable and happy existence, lived, like a Philosopher, at the farther end of Champagne, in a small house, two leagues from Rheims; he had been a widower several years, and found in the study of science, and his tenderness for an only son, amusements and happiness equal to his wishes.

When young Luzincourt had attained his nineteenth year, his father told him of his design to send him to Strasbourg. My son, said he, you are not a gentleman, and have no fortune; I have given you an education which will procure you the means of distinguishing yourself, if you have activity and a noble ambition. You have reason and understanding, and yet I do not ask-what condition of

life

life you would prefer, nor fhall I make a choice for you myfelf.

My parents, without confulting my inclinations, made me a lawyer ; probity preferved me from the dreadful mifery of being a bad Magiftrate ; but I did not love my profeffion, and my inclination for fcience made me quit it at forty. During twenty years, I fulfilled duties which, to me, were painful ; and when I wholly addicted myfelf to the ftudies to which my genius led me, I was too old to become eminent in a new career.

This experience, and the reflections I had made, have prevented me from preffing the choice of a profeffion upon you, till you fhould arrive at that age when your powers and propenfities fhould be developed. At prefent I will fend you to Strafbourg, where I would have you pafs two years in the fchools where law is taught, becaufe there is no condition of life in which a knowledge of the laws is not ufeful, and even neceffary to a good citizen.

Young Luzincourt affured his father of his obedience ; and three days after this converfation, departed for Strafbourg. Arrived in Alface, he purfued his ftudies with ardour, writ regularly to his father, and, in the account he gave him of his occupations and amufements, continually fpoke of
the

the inexpreffible pleafure he took in reading Dramatic Authors and Works of Morality.

Luzincourt alfo kept up a correfpondence with
a friend, of his own age, who lived at Rheims.
The name of this young man was Damoville:
he was the eldeft fon of his father's moft intimate
friend, and having been educated together, he
had conceived the moft tender friendfhip for Damoville.

Never, however, did convenience and habit form
a connexion lefs liable to laft. Luzincourt, naturally timid and thoughtful, fpoke little, was diffident
of himfelf, and having, with much modefty, a great
defire to gain information, he was filent, without
an effort, and liftened with avidity. To this referve, this attention to the difcourfe of others, he
was indebted for penetration much fuperior to his
years. He already poffeffed the ufeful art of reading the countenance, and eafily tracing there the
flighteft expreffion of envy, difdain, or ill humour;
nature had given him a difcerning mind, a delicate
tafte, a lively imagination, a feeling heart, and a
noble foul.

Damoville, on the contrary, full of confidence
and pride, fpoke with affurance, and heard without
attention; his head was hot, and his heart cold;
his ideas often dazzled, but were often unjuft and
inconfiftent;

inconsistent ; without sensibility, without greatness of soul, incapable of reflecting, of meditating, he imagined heroism, of all kind, to be either the effect of self-interested calculation, or the fruit of folly, more proper to excite the pity, than merit the admiration of a Philosopher.

Though his self-love was excessive, his society was not without charms; his pliability was wonderful, and taught him to take, with ease, a thousand different forms. Having neither principles nor fixed character, he could change his opinion with facility, and this often preserved him from that obstinacy which pride usually inspires. Equally inconsistent and indiscreet, his defects sometimes gave his conduct and discourse an agreeable appearance of frankness and originality; and he possessed a certain natural malignity, which never appeared but in the form of a joke, and which might easily be taken for gaiety and good-humour.

Luzincourt, notwithstanding his penetration, did not know Damoville : accustomed from his tenderest infancy to look upon him as his brother, he could not judge impartially, but was equally blind to his sentiments and character ; he wrote to him with pleasure and punctuality, gave him a circumstantial history of his occupations, and Damoville, on his part, informed Luzincourt, that he, likewise, had a passionate love for reading ; and

told

told him, moreover, in confidence, he had already begun to compose. Luzincourt, in his answers, exhorted him not to be too hasty; but notwithstanding this prudent advice, Damoville replied, that, hurried on by the fire of imagination, he wrote, he composed continually, and every month enriched *Le Mercure de France* (*a*) with some new production.

The time being ended, prescribed by his father, Luzincourt quitted Strasbourg and returned to Champagne; his joy was great, at finding himself once more in the arms of his father, and in the company of Damoville. My friend, said the latter to him, the die is cast, and my life shall be consecrated to the service of the Muses; my father consents; the success of my last Ode, and especially of my Philosophic Tale, has determined him to send me to Paris.

Paris! What by yourself?

Certainly; but I am known there to the most distinguished men of letters. I had the precaution to praise them, with some address, in my Ode, and my Philosophic Tale is full of touches purposely meant to please them. ——Besides, they are astonished, that a young man, of my age, should have been

----

(*a*) *A kind of Weekly Magazine, published at Paris, in which the Moral Tales of Marmontel first appeared.* T.

been the Author of two productions fo full of genius.——I have received letters from three of them, which I will fhew thee. They exhort me to quit the country; they expect, they wifh to fee me, and I fhall be gone in two months time.

The fame evening Damoville fhewed his friend the letters of which he had fpoken, which really contained the moft flattering eulogium on the talents of Damoville, and efpecially on his Philofophic Tale. Luzincourt could fcarcely conceal his furprize: he had read this vaunted Tale, and well remembered, that certain works, and certain Academicians, were praifed in it very emphatically; but he likewife remembered, he had never read any thing more uniformly dull.

As he was modeft and inexperienced, he fuppofed himfelf wrong; he had judged Damoville, in the bottom of his heart, to be abfolutely devoid of genius. I was deceived, faid he, and I am happy to find I was. Damoville will become famous in the noble, the brilliant courfe he is about to run; it is proper, and moft pleafing to be proud of the fame of a friend.

Luzincourt, when interrogated by his father, freely confefied that he, as well as Damoville, had a ftrong propenfity to the Belles-Lettres; but, added he, I am not ignorant, my inclination cannot fupply the want of talents. I have not the

proud

proud hope of becoming hereafter, equal to the authors I so much admire; the title of an estimable writer may satisfy my ambition, and is the wish of my heart. Speak then, my father, you can guide, you can instruct me; should you not approve the choice I have made, I will relinquish it instantly.

No, my son, said his father, tenderly embracing him, I will not speak against what I approve. Go, then, with Damoville; gain instruction, there, where genius and the fine arts are understood and admired; only be careful to preserve your character, your principles, and your morals; look, reflect, before you write; examine nature, and your own heart; above all things, be consistent and declaim not against intolerance, while you detest and persecute those who adopt not your opinions: vaunt not the consolations of philosophy while criticism offends, while contradiction irritates, and truth is disagreeable to you; pretend not to the sublime title of a Philosopher, if you cannot yourself afford a noble example of justice, moderation, and fortitude, or if you cannot pardon and contemn cabal and intrigue.

But I am undisturbed on that head, I know your sentiments, my son; they will beget reputation and fame. Even without genius, and with a common mind, you might speak worthily of Vir-

tue,

tue, whose image is always impreſt on a generous
and pure heart; but you, I hope, ſhall ſhew her in all
her beauty ; ſhall demonſtrate her to be invariable
and real ; ſhall give her Religion for her baſis, and
ſhall paint her under a form ſo benevolent, ſo
perfect, ſo natural, that the very Atheiſt ſhall be
forced to admire, and bluſh he had before time
miſtaken her.

Young Luzincourt promiſed to follow his father's counſels, and endeavour to juſtify his hopes :
he remained another month in the country, and
then departed with Damoville for Paris, where he
lodged at the houſe of a relation, a celebrated Advocate, and Damoville hired a ſmall apartment in
the ſame ſtreet.

The very day after his arrival, Damoville ſought
out all the men of letters from whom he had received ſuch flattering anſwers ; his reception equalled his hopes, and they propoſed he ſhould take a
department in a Journal ; they informed him of the
principles it was neceſſary he ſhould adopt, and
Damoville ſhewed all the condeſcenſion they could
hope, whence they immediately predicted his progreſs would be great and glorious.

While Damoville, devoted to his new patrons,
indulged the moſt dazzling hopes, Luzincourt
led a very different life. Darnay, the Advocate,
his relation, with whom he lodged, had married
the

the Sister of a celebrated Painter, and was visited by many of the best Artists. A society, like this, was perfectly conformable to the taste of Luzin-court, who naturally loved the arts, and felt how necessary it was for a man of letters to obtain well-founded knowledge on such noble subjects. He had learnt to draw, understood music, and listened with attention, and a strong desire of in-struction, to the conversations he so frequently heard: he became particularly intimate with many of the Artists, went to see them when at work, and accompanied them when they visited the galleries of the Louvre, the Luxembourg, and the collec-tions of private persons.

Such were his morning employments: his after-noons were spent in attending the Theatres; and, at his return, before he went to bed, in writing a Journal of every thing interesting he had heard or seen in the course of the day.

In the midst of these amusements, he was afflicted to find he no more saw Damoville, who had been entirely lost to him for three months past; his at-tempts to draw him to the house of Darnay were ineffectual. Damoville loved to talk, to dissertate, to shine, and not to be instructed. The company that met at Darnay's tired him, he came once, but never returned.

Vanity,

Vanity, however, at length brought him back to Luzincourt. He had formed a very false opinion of the latter, with respect to himself; he supposed him to entertain a high idea of his merit; pride cannot feel, cannot understand true friendship. Damoville imagined its looks, its delicate attentions and cares, to which the heart gave birth, were only so many homages to, so many avowals of, his superiority, and the tenderest of friends, in his eyes, was but his admirer.

Damoville, at last, found it necessary, to his vanity, to inform Luzincourt of his new success. Accordingly, one morning, he went to excuse and justify himself for his long neglect, when he gave a pompous detail of the occupations which overwhelmed him, the works he had in hand, and renewed his assurances of an entire and unbounded friendship.

Luzincourt was moved, and Damoville coming to the point, said to him, I will prove to thee how great, how sincere my confidence in thee is, by telling thee exactly of all that affects me nearest; here, my friend, look, I have brought thee an Epistle, in verse, addressed to *the Philosopher of Ferney*, (M. de Voltaire) not yet printed. It is about three weeks since I sent it him, and I have received, this very morning, an answer from

him

him, in verse, which thou shalt hear, presently; listen first to my Epistle.

Damoville then took his manuscript from his pocket, and read in a loud voice, a long, tiresome Epistle, dictated, from one end to the other, by the most open flattery. *The Philosopher of Ferney*, however, compared the talents of Damoville to those of *La Fare* and *Chaulieu*. Damoville, said he, has their grace and ease, without their negligence and defects.

Luzincourt, surprized and confounded, was silent. Damoville talked on; thou mayest well suppose, said he, I shall print both my Epistle and his Reply.

Indeed! I would not advise you.

No! Why so, prithee?

It does not seem, to me, proper to print one's own eulogium.

Oh! do not fear; this is a well established custom. An Author may not only print, without scruple, verse and prose in his praise, but he may cite, in his preface, the agreeable things he has heard of himself; nay, if he has genius, may even invent some happy reply, which is commonly attributed to some person whom he protects, or some friend who is now no more. If these little freedoms were not permitted, how might such brilliant

liant

liant reputations, as are daily formed, be fo foon acquired.

I confefs, I fcarcely can comprehend how an Author may difcover fuch exceffive vanity, without difgufting the public.

Well, and where is the harm ?——The public is difgufted, and blames the Author who praifes himfelf; but while he is blamed he is believed. The modeft Author and the vain, are, equally, taken at their words. Be humble, and you will be thought juft to your own abilities ; dare boldly to praife yourfelf, and the world will be of your opinion ; you will be called proud, but you will be admired.

If fuch be your opinion of the public, you can hardly be vain of its fuffrage.——Wherefore do men of letters labour ? Is it not to enlighten mankind ? Is it not to merit the world's efteem and gratitude ?

Such are the motives given in a preface ; but furely thou art not fimple enough to believe them. Men write to obtain a name, becaufe celebrity leads to wealth : not to mention one is proud of the homage of the very fools one defpifes.——But let us return to my Epiftle, how doft thou like it ?

You feem to me too prodigal of praife.

How

How so? Is it possible to praise the Author of *Alzira*, *Mahomet*, and so many other dramatic master-pieces too much?

Certainly not; there are no praises in this respect, which his genius does not justify; but you give him the title of Philosopher and Sage, which he never can deserve. Is he superior to the foibles which envy, hatred, and resentment produce? Is he even peaceable and happy?——He is benevolent——he makes a noble use of his riches——but he has defamed, he has blackened his enemies.

His writings breathe the very spirit of philosophy, and have produced a revolution which has——

Destroyed Religion, and corrupted Morality.

No man has better defended the rights of humanity.

You forget that he was preceded by *Fenelon*. You do not hold it possible, that an Author's sole design should be to benefit mankind.——Read Telemachus, once more; a work written to instruct Kings, and enlighten the world, and think better. I should be sorry for you, could you prefer the declamations and epigrams of Voltaire, to such a sublime system of morality.

You may say what you please, but you will never rob Voltaire of the glory of having been the

firſt

firſt poet who ſpoke the language of reaſon and philoſophy.

I am ſorry you have not found the language of reaſon in the works of Boileau, and many other Authors.——But what think you of Pope ? Is not he the Poet of Philoſophy ? What philoſophic Piece has Voltaire ever produced, any way equal to the ESSAY ON MAN ?

You will not at leaſt deny, that the abilities of Voltaire are aſtoniſhingly extenſive, or that he has not a univerſal genius ?

What do you mean by a univerſal genius ?

A man who is ſuperior in every ſpecies of Literature. I am willing to allow (between ourſelves) that Voltaire is not what he has, perhaps, been too haſtily called, the Conqueror of two Rivals who reigned over the Theatre ; but what tragic author, of *this age*, can be called his equal ?

None ; not even the author of *Rhadamiſtus* and *Electra*. Crebillon, no doubt, had genius, but he has only written two pieces worthy the ſtage. Although Piron wrote *la Metromanie*, he muſt not be compared to Moliere ; nor have thoſe more reaſon, in my opinion, who would equal Crebillon to Voltaire.

What ſay you to his hiſtory ?

His Hiſtory of Charles XII. is an agreeable romance, and his Age of Louis XIV. dazzles the imagination.

imagination. But are they written in the ſtyle of Hiſtory? What can you ſay to a writer, who is always partial, always paſſionate, guided by the ſpirit of party, and unceaſingly ſacrificing reaſon, morality, and truth, to private views, perſonal intereſt, and a vain deſire to ſhine.

You, no doubt, think his fugitive pieces deteſtable too?

No; ſome of them are charming; but he is here ſurpaſſed by *Greſſet*, whoſe Verſes, as witty as thoſe of Voltaire, have a thouſand times more ſweetneſs and harmony; nor can you mention one fugitive piece, by the latter, which may juſtly be preferred to the *Chartreuſe* (*a*), or *l'Epître ſur la Convaleſcence* (*b*).

And you think nothing of Voltaire's gaiety?

What gaity!——Deprive him of the deſire to blacken, to avenge himſelf of, to ridicule, his enemies, and give him, in it's ſtead, reaſon, decency, and reſpect for religion, and you will rob him of all his pretended gaiety, which is only inſpired by impiety, malignity, and a contempt for morals. He never knew the art of laughing with innocence; and his natural gaiety is ſo confined, that, notwithſtanding the ſuperiority of his wit, he never attempted to be pleaſant, without offence to

religion

(*a*) The Charter-houſe, or Carthuſian Monaſtry.
(*b*) An Epiſtle on the King's recovery.

religion and modesty, but he was dull.   He
has written the *Gardeufe de Caffette* (a) ;——and
has given the stage *Un Fier en Fat* (b), and a *Madame de Croupillac.*

Oh ! I give up his Comedies—Nay, his Operas
——He has not succeeded in Lyric Poetry, I own.
But what do you say to his Henriade ?

That it contains fine paffages, and that I should
admire it, could I read it through without an effort.

If that work be not unequalled, you cannot deny
but Voltaire has the merit of having written the
only Epic Poem in our language.

And what think you is the reason? It is becaufe Poets of genius have always preferred
the writing of Tragedies.   An Epic Poem demands deep study, and great length of time ; and
the glory which is acquired, by writing it, is rather
durable than noify ; while the applaufes, obtained on
the Theatre, are more flattering, and more condu-
cive to fortune.   I willingly allow, that a fublime
Poem, fuch, for example, as Paradife Loft, is, of
all others, a work which requires the moft genius.
But I muft likewife think, that he who could write
a good Tragedy, might write as good a Poem as
the Henriade.

(a) The Keeper of the Cafket.
(b) A haughty Fool.

G 2

Well,

Well, but do not you admire the aftonifhing union of wit and fcience in Voltaire?

Fontenelle was a man of wit, infinitely more learned than Voltaire (*a*); the latter will never be thought a great Mathematician, and he was a very bad experimental Philofopher; he was ignorant of the firft Elements of Chymiftry, and every thing he faid, on Natural Hiftory, is equally void of reafon and truth, and demonftrative of his profound ignorance on that fubject. He has fpoken too on the Arts, but without loving or underftanding them (*b*). Afk the Artifts, and they will tell you, he had neither tafte, difcernment, nor knowledge of them. Hence it is very true that Voltaire has had the puerile and ambitious pretenfion to appear univerfal, when he was fuperior only in one fpecious of writing. It feems to me, too, that his profe writings evidently prove he had but one manner, and that he could not vary his ftyle with his fubjed. Was it Hiftory, a Novel, a Letter, it was all the fame: his partizans called this furprizing uniformity, *the fignature of Voltaire*, and think they praife him when they fay, they can find

(*a*) M. de Fontenelle was a Member of the Academy of Sciences; nobody yet ever thonght of beftowing that honour on Voltaire.

(*b*) He, himfelf, has faid, he did not tafte the beauties of Painting and Mufic.

find him in a Billet, and cannot miftake his hand : they forgot he is only fo fure to be found, becaufe he had but one manner ; and that, becaufe, during fixty years, he continually repeated the fame witticifms, and the fame declamations. Montef- quieu has only written three works, and has each time had the happy art, which tafte and genius alone may give, to change his tone, and feize the ftyle beft fuited to his different fubjects. No one can fay, they find, in the Temple of Gnidus, the *figna- ture* of the author of the Spirit of Laws; though it is certain, that in Zadig you cannot miftake the hand which traced the Univerfal Hiftory. May a man pretend to univerfal genius, becaufe he gives a different title to each volume he writes ? Cer- tainly not. A multitude of volumes will but dif- cover fuch pretenfions to be ill founded ; while, on the contrary, one fole work may difplay a won- derful variety of talents. The illuftrious Author of *The Hiftory of Nature*, M. de Buffon, has proved that one man may unite vaft know- ledge, a brilliant imagination, and the enchanting art of painting and defcribing, with equal fupe- riority, the affecting, the awful, the majeftic, and the terrible. In his work we find the moft perfect examples and varieties of eloquence ; Poet, Painter, profound Metaphyfician, fublime Philo- fopher ; each, in turn : his pliant and extenfive

G 3

genius

genius embraces, and adapts itself to all. It gives, with the fame facility, the moft delicate touches to the fhorteft details, while it conceives a plan the moft extenfive and vaft; no French writer ever better underftood his own language; none ever joined fo much precifion with fo much eloquence, or was equally correct and equally bril-liant.

We are agreed on that head, replied Damoville; nay, I confefs, I have always thought that an Author, who is fuperior in one branch of literature, might eafily write, fuccefsfully, at leaft, in various others.

Nothing can be more true, replied Luzincourt. If, for example, Racine had lived as long as Vol-taire, with the fame defire of being thought a univerfal genius, can it be doubted, that the Author of Athalia and Britannicus would not have written Hiftory in a fublime ftyle: he, who knew fo well the human heart, who painted, with fo much ftrength and truth, the paffion and jealoufy of Phædra and Roxana; the matrimonial tender-nefs of Clytemneftra; the affecting love of Be-renice; the fury of Hermione; could not he have written an interefting Novel, or a fentimental Comedy, equal to *Nanine*, *L'Efcoffoife*, and *Charlot*, think you? The tender, the elegant Racine, had he written Operas, would he have been inferior to
Quinault?

Quinault? He poſſeſſed the difficult art of criti-
cifing, with taſte, and of delicate raillery. He
has left us ſome letters, in which we find all the
ſoft, all the witty and ſatirical irony, which gave
ſo juſt a reputation to the *Lettres Provinciales*;
and as to gaiety, real and frank gaiety, who ſhall
diſpute it with the author of the Plaideurs? What
then ſhall we ſay to the great Corneille, firſt Sovereign and true Legiſlator of the Theatre; he
who created the two ſpecies worthy to illuſtrate
and reign over the ſtage, Tragedy and Comedy (*a*).
He has raviſhed from Moliere the glory of giving
his nation the firſt good characteriſtic Comedy; and
when Racine appeared, France was in poſſeſſion of
all the great works of Corneille (*b*).

To

(*a*) And even the heroic Comedy, likewiſe: Don San-
cho of Aragon, is the firſt piece that was written of the
kind; and it ought to be remarked too, that Corneille
ſucceeded, to perfection, in Lyric Poetry.

(*b*) M. de Fontenelle has obſerved, Corneille had no
preceding Author to guide him, but that Racine had
Corneille: if this creates an immenſe diſtance between
Corneille and Racine, what muſt it do in the caſe of
Voltaire, who had both Racine and Corneille? Neither
has he neglected to profit by their works, as much as
poſſible; he has taken a great number of lines from them
both; has imitated their characters, their ſituations, and
their very ſubjects. Thus, it is to Polyeucte we owe the

G 4   Orphan

To speak truth, replied Damoville, I am partly of thy opinion; it is not possible, in reality, to compare Voltaire to Corneille and Racine; but the former has had the art to raise a party in his favour, which cannot at present be withstood; besides that, by the freedom and frivolity of his writings, he has seduced the world in general, and we must swim with the stream.

Do you believe that Reputation, acquired by cabal and intrigue, can be lasting?

It is the soonest established, which is the thing most essential. Life is short, its duration uncertain, and extravagance only would patiently expect a desired blessing, which activity and address might presently obtain.

But

Orphan of China. In Polyeucte, Pauline relates how she once loved Severus; but he, being then poor, was rejected by her parents, who forced her to mary Polyeucte; that she, since, has become fond of, and truly attached to, her husband; and that she is greatly distressed lest Severus, now become powerful, should revenge himself on Polyeucte. Idamé, in the Orphan of China, says exactly the same thing. Gengiskan, formerly the obscure Temugin, was rejected by her parents; he now returns, armed with power, and she is in the utmost fear for her spouse, &c. Many like examples, equally striking, might be cited; and for the satisfaction of youth, we shall some time enter more fully into these sort of subjects.

But what is this defired blefling ?

Perfonal refpect, honours and wealth.

What do you call perfonal refpect ?

I wifh to be one of the heads of the prevailing Party: to have Friends, Partifans, Puffers, Dependents, Enemies.

Wifh to have enemies ?

No doubt——It is neceflary to have a right to fay in Society, or in a Preface, *my Enemies*; they are ufeful to a man of letters, and give him an opportunity, whenever he thinks proper, to intereft the world in his behalf, by calling himfelf a perfecuted man ; and artfully hinting, that he is only hated becaufe he is envied. I own the thought has been hacknied a little, but, yet, fo happy a one, that it ftill retains its former force, and is every day repeated with the fame fuccefs. In fhort, there are a thoufand circumftances under which our enemies may be called our beft friends. A Poem not read, a Comedy damned, or any like difgrace, may be laid to their charge, *it is all the effect of party.*

You would only fhine then for a moment ?

I trouble not myfelf about Reputation after I am dead. An oppofite conduct might, perhaps, better obtain the praifes of pofterity ; but I fet little value on fuch praife, give me prefent enjoyment. I am of thofe, who, by a calculation fomewhat felfifh, but

moft

moſt philoſophic, wiſh to be rich while they live, and who would not heſitate to purchaſe a mere Life-annuity. I neither love nor eſteen men ſuffi-ciently, to form the romantic project of exiſting for their ſakes; and they treat thoſe infinitely better by whom they are amuſed, nay deceived, than thoſe by whom they are inſtructed.

The writer who wearies his Readers, is always in the wrong; truth ſhould ever wear an agreeable dreſs; but feeling can embelliſh, can ſoften the auſterity of morals, and give charms to the leſſons of wiſdom.

Yes; and the world will then think lightly of the Moraliſt, will place him in the claſs of Novel Writers.

If they place him by the ſide of Richardſon, the Author may conſole himſelf.

To appear profound in the eye of the public, you ought to be dull.

But you will not be read.

But you will be admired; and a ſingle work, of this kind, is enough to eſtabliſh a reputation.

You are joking to be ſure.

I never was more ſerious. I will give you an unanſwerable proof.——We are alone, and I can depend on thy diſcretion.

Whither does this preamble lead?

Shouldſt

Shouldst thou reveal what I am going to confide to thee, I should lofe my Protectors, my Friends, and all my hopes, beyond retrieving.

I need not make proteftations, Damoville.

Well then, there is a little work fo fingularly cold, fo dreadfully dull, that it is impoffible to have the fortitude to read it through in one day, though it is not above fixty pages; not but it has fome rationality, and a few ingenious ideas; but its ftyle is fo heavy, fo diffufe, fo incorrect, fo deftitute of purity, feeling, and elegance, that it does not contain a fingle paffage worthy of citation, and yet it is in the higheft vogue; but why, becaufe the Author has many friends who have puffed and cried up this production. After all the praifes they have heard of it, nobody dare own how intolerably infipid they found it; but every one repeats, by rote, *It is a wonderful production*; thofe even who never went farther than the firft page, and who know nothing more of it than it's title, do not fail to confirm this judgment; and thus it is that thefe Echoes of Echoes, by a repetition of the fame found, confer univerfal fame. This is the reafon, my friend, why I give into intrigue and party fpirit, and why I fo highly efteem the praifes of the Philofopher of Ferney.

Can fuch praifes give pleafure? Has he not lavifhed them all the days of his life, on medio-

crity?

crity? Could ever he refolve to give Genius it's due? Recollect his notes upon Corneille, which we read together at Rheims with fo much indignation. Remember what he has faid of Crebillon, Jean-Baptifte Rouffeau, Boileau, and La Fontaine (*a*). Knoweft thou not his reiterated attempts, in profe and verfe, to diminifh the glory of the Author of Telemachus? Art thou ignorant of his hatred of Montefquieu, and how often he has attacked his works? Or wouldft thou dare affirm in his prefence, that Jean-Jaques Rouffeau was a man of genius? Haft thou not read that horrid Libel, that fhameful Monument of the blackeft, the meaneft envy——

Nay, be calm, my good friend: I am perfectly acquainted with all this. But what then? I am unknown, I want fupport; his protection is not only ufeful, but abfolutely neceffary, and muft, if poffible, be obtained. Befides, you cannot fuppofe, but that people of fuperior merit may be found among his moft zealous Partifans.

Moft certainly, I could name feveral.

Well, I fhall deferve a place in this fmall clafs.

But

(*a*) See the notes to Voltaire's age of Louis XIV. La Fontaine, he fays, has but one fole charm, that of being unaffected, natural. (*Celui du naturel*).

But Voltaire is eighty years old; and fhall not this party, the authority of which thou feemeft to revere, which has but a moment to exift, and which has already loft much of its weight, fhall it not die with it's Chief?

Darnay entered the chamber as Luzincourt was fpeaking, which put an end to a converfation that gave birth to the moft melancholy reflections, in the breaft of Luzincourt, concerning the character of his friend.

Damoville returned, fome days after this, and propofed to prefent Luzincourt, where the beft company in Paris, as he faid, affembled every evening. The miftrefs of the houfe, added he, is an old woman, the widow of a Financier; fhe is faid to have been celebrated in her youth for fome dozen adventures, rather of the fcandalous than the romantic kind; but now, returned to reafon and fociety, fhe lives, philofophically, in the happy calm of the paffions. The remembrance fhe pre-ferves of her ancient errors, gives her an indul-gence towards the wanderings of youth, which it is impoffible to carry further; nobody can be more tolerant, therefore, by way of juft gratitude; others readily overlook her unbounded love of Pha-raoh, and a few tricking liberties, which to be fure fhe rather too often permits herfelf to take.

And

And does this woman fee the beft company of Paris, fayeft thou?

To be fure fhe does; fhe has a good houfe, and keeps an excellent table, and what could you wifh for more?

I have heard there are women almoft as contemptible as her you have defcribed, who have not been fhut out of fociety; but then I always underftood they were women of high birth, and fuppofed that, out of refpect to an illuftrious family, it was poffible the world might not do itfelf juftice on fuch a kind of perfon, when fhe happens to poffefs great wealth, wit, and agreeable manners.

Pfhaw, my dear Luzincourt, the world is not fo nice. Madame de Surval is fifty-five years of age, talkative, tirefome, and without common fenfe, and yet thou fhalt meet *all France* at her houfe. Shall I take thee thither this evening?

You cannot pleafe me more. I have a ftrong defire to fee and know the world; though I am fenfible of my awkwardnefs and timidity, and how ignorant I am of its cuftoms.

Read, attentively, the works of the younger Crebillon. I acknowledge they are contemptible, but they have one ineftimable merit, they contain a true picture of fafhionable life.

I cannot believe it; I do not know the world, but good fenfe tells me, it is impoffible vice fhould

dare

dare fo impudently to fhew itfelf with impunity ; it can only be tolerated when it is difguifed ; no man may feduce every woman he meets, by openly difcovering a perverfe mind, and the groffeft ftupidity; nor can I imagine, that felf-fufficiency, and ill-bred familiarity, are the manners of fafhionable people.

But how does it happen thy prejudices do not vanifh, when thou feeft that almoft all Authors, who have defcribed the fafhionable world, agree with Crebillon? Thou thinkeft highly, for example, of the Moral Tales of Marmontel.

I do; but, in my opinion, they are far from being all *moral*. The Author himfelf, in his preface, owns, that Laufus and Lydia, the Shepherdefs of the Alps, Annette and Lubin, and the Marriages of the Samnites, are not moral Tales; nor do I think that By Good Luck, is more moral; nay, I own, I cannot fee the moral purpofes of the Scruple, the Sylph-Hufband, Soliman II. and Friendfhip put to the Teft; nothing, I think, can be lefs moral than that of Alcibiades, Lauretta, and the Four Phials.

I own the defcriptions, in thefe Tales, are fomewhat lively, and poffefs more fpirit than decency; but the queftion is not whether the title and the work correfpond, it is to know whether the

Author

Author agrees with Crebillon in his Picture of the World.

But who pretends to deny that the general conversations, the scenes of fashionable life, the phrases of the characters in *Les Egaremens du Cœur & de L'Esprit* (*a*), have the most striking similarity with pictures of the same kind, drawn in the Moral Tales?

Well, and thou wilt not deny that it is universally acknowledged the Moral Tales present a true picture of manners?

Universally acknowledged! I know not that; I know it is not doubted in the country, but the opinion of fashionable people must decide on this subject.

Marmontel is worthy of the best company.

He is so; but Crebillon never lived among fashionable people; how then could he know their manners? Is it not, therefore, rational to conclude, that the Author of the Moral Tales has, in this instance, been contented to imitate, instead of copying after nature.

The most convincing argument will be to shew thee the world, and thou wilt then soon change thy opinion.

If the world thou speakest of, be such as it is described in these works, I shall soon quit it; it

(*a*) The Wanderings of the Heart and Mind.

will

will not be worth the trouble of studying : not to mention, if its characters be thus grosly ridiculous and vicious, it need no great sagacity to quickly understand it.

Damoville took Luzincourt the same evening to the house of Madame de Surval; there was much company and much play, the visit was short, and Luzincourt saw nothing remarkable. Curiosity soon brought him there again, and, to oblige Damoville, Madame de Surval often invited him to stay supper; during which time, he had an opportunity of observing scenes which, to him, were totally new. His surprize, indeed, was extreme, when he found that the Authors whom he had accused of not knowing the world, had given but a too faithful Picture, though with strong touches, of what he now saw.

Among the ladies who visited Madame de Surval, there were three or four of families sufficiently distinguished to be generally known, and these appeared intimately acquainted with the rest.

As to the men, Luzincourt often met men eminent for their birth, titles, and employments; wherefore he could not doubt that the society in which he was, must be what is called *Good Company*.

The success of Damoville, in this Society, was prodigious; especially among the ladies. He
made

made Verſes, Extempores, Impromptus, ſpoke with confidence, and totally eclipſed Luzincourt, who began to ſhake off his timidity, but not his reſerve.

Among the many who frequented this houſe, Luzincourt diſtinguiſhed a man who appeared evidently ſuperior to the reſt ; and who likewiſe, on his part, knew how to eſtimate Luzincourt. He was called the Viſcount de Valrive, was about four or five and thirty, had an intereſting and intelligent countenance, a noble air, a cool politeneſs, and converſed with eaſe and underſtanding. Luzincourt eaſily perceived the particular reaſon which brought him to the houſe of Madame de Surval : he was in love with a lady named Madame d'Herblay.

Luzincourt obſerved, in the conduct of the Viſcount, ſomething unaccountably odd ; he was continually changing his manner : with Luzincourt and two or three more, who came there but ſeldom, he was amiable and communicative, and diſcovered equal wit and good underſtanding ; with a great number of others he was cold and ſilent ; and when he ſpoke to the women, he inſtantly became trifling, familiar, and ironical ; eſpecially when he addreſſed himſelf to the lady, concerning whom he ſeemed moſt intereſted.

Not-

Notwithstanding this apparent inconsistency, Luzincourt found his secret inclinations for the Viscount strengthen, daily in his heart, and daily increase ; their sympathy was mutual, though Luzincourt had never yet had any occasion of conversing with the Viscount at his ease ; that is to say, without others mixing in the conversation. Chance, at last, gave him the opportunity he wished ; the Viscount one evening would not sup, and Luzincourt remained alone with him, while the company sat down to table.

I am quite happy, said the Viscount, to have an hour's conversation with you. You have interested my heart in your behalf ; permit me to ask you a few questions. I need not demand what profession in life you intend to follow ; that you love Literature, and cultivate the Belles Lettres with success, is evident ; but wherefore do you come here ?

I wish to study, to know the world.

That study can only be interesting in good company, which you certainly cannot find here.

How so ? Do I not find you here ?

Men of my age, may, without danger, permit themselves these little liberties ; the motives of coming here must be either curiosity, a passion for play, idleness, or some momentary whim ;

and

and it is for this reason you sometimes meet men
of fashion here.

But what brings the women?

The women! There is not one who comes here,
would be admitted in good company.

And yet there are three or four whose births
might entitle them to that honour.

And did, in their early youth; but they have
long been banished; a husband, justly irritated,
has two modes of punishing a guilty wife; he can
shut her up in a convent, or come to a public
separation. In the latter case, he delivers her up
to the justice of Society, which never fails to reject
her, especially if she does not find, in an illustrious
and respected family, some very zealous protectors.
In this case, if the unfortunate wife has any feeling
left, she flies into some distant province, and there
conceals her shame and sorrow; but if her passions,
while they lead her astray, have debased her mind,
she then remains at Paris, audaciously braves
public contempt, and renders herself completely
odious, by exciting the indignation and hatred
which effrontery and avowed wickedness always
inspire. She must see Company, however, and
she wishes it should be numerous, select it cannot
be; she, therefore, unites with all the women,
who have, like her, been excluded Good Company,
and with many others, who never had admission

to

to it; and thus she passes her life, in three or four houses similar to this we are in; falls into the established manners, and endeavours to distinguish herself by malignity, equal to the badness of her morals, to revenge herself of the circles whence she is proscribed; her calumnies cost her nothing, and she would persuade the world, that the women who refuse her acquaintance, are as contemptible as herself; and thus she defames every woman, without distinction, or the appearance of probability.

And so then, cried Luzincourt, with an air of the utmost satisfaction, I am, at present, in very bad company.

You are indeed, replied the Viscount, laughing; nor do you seem to be sorry for the discovery.

Sorry! I am transported!——And the works, which we country folks suppose to be a picture of life and manners, paint only what is to be seen here.

Merely so; but look, yonder is a volume of Marmontel's Tales, let us read a description or two of this kind, and I am sure you will find he has exaggerated, even after what you have here observed.

The Viscount took the book, opened it at a venture, and said, Ay, here is the Good Mother: This tale is one of those in which there is most character and description of the world. Do you recollect the subject?

Very

Very confusedly.

It is a tender and virtuous mother, dedicating herself to the education of her daughter; two persons pretend to the honour of being Emily's husband. The one is a man of prudence and understanding, the other a Coxcomb, who loses no opportunity of speaking, without disguise, his mean and unnatural sentiments, or of shewing his contempt of morals and decency. The Author calls this odious and ridiculous person, *The dangerous Verglan*, and, without giving this character the trouble of feigning a passion he does not feel, makes him beloved by the modest and sensible Emily; the mother easily discovers her daughter's secret, but certain that Emily will in time despise Verglan, she continues to grant him admission to her house. Let us read a passage.

" The arrangement of Count d'Auberive with
" his Lady, was at that time the town-talk; it was
" said that, after a very sharp quarrel, and bitter
" complains, on both sides, of mutual infidelity,
" they ended, by owning neither of them were
" indebted to the other, and laughing at their
" folly for having fallen out, and been jealous
" without being in love; that the Count had
" consented to let his wife retain the Chevalier
" de Clange as her lover; and she, on her part,
" promised to receive the Marchioness de Talbe,

to

" to whom her hufband paid his addreffes, with
" all the cordiality poffible; that peace had thus
" been ratified over a fupper, and that, being all
" come to *a right underftanding*, never were feen
" two happier pair of lovers.——Verglan, at
" hearing this recital, exclaimed, nothing could be
" more prudent."

It is proper to remark, faid the Vifcount, interrupting himfelf, that Emily is prefent, and does
not lofe a word of this converfation; and likewife
to inform you, that, among good company, this
never could happen to a young unmarried woman.
No mother would fuffer a converfation fo fcandalous before her daughter, nor could the moft inconfiderate or depraved man be tempted to forget
the refpect due to youth and innocence. This,
therefore, is abfolutely contrary to our manners:
nor does the ftory of Auberive depict them better.
We find eafy hufbands in the world who know
their difgrace, yet feem not to regard it; but
there is no example to be found, like what the
Author of the Moral Tales calls the *arrangement*
of the Marquis of Auberive with his lady, or of
hufband and wife confiding their mutual infide-
lities to each other, ending their jealous quarrels
by laughing at their folly, ratifying peace over a
fupper, and coming to a *right underftanding* in
prefence of the miftrefs and gallant. Such a picture

ture is as chimerical as it is revolting; the world may be brought to pardon those who go aftray, but never thofe who debafe themfelves; deliberate inde-cency, and total neglect of propriety, is a wrong that never can be repaired.

But let us purfue the conduct of the ftory. Verglan, during a long converfation, continues to maintain that Auberive has acted very wifely; fays that, formerly, a hufband became the ridiculous object of public contempt at madam's firft falfe ftep; approves the prefent manners, makes an eu-logium on perjury and adultery, and concludes by faying, it is thefe things that make him defirous of being married.

His rival, Belzor, combats thefe opinions with feeling and underftanding. Emily liftens, and her mother now and then throws in a reflection. At length the Marquis of Auberive is announced, and juft at this place let us read another page.

" Ah, Marquis, thou art come quite a-propos,
" faid Verglan. Prithee tell us, is this ftory true?
" Thefe good folks here pretend, that thy wife has
" given thee rhubarb, and thou haft fent back
" fenna.

" Pfhaw! nonfenfe! faid Auberive, indolently.

" I affirm nothing would be more prudent than
" thy conduct, continued Verglan; but Belzor here
" condemns thee without appeal——

" Why

" Why so ? Would not he have done the same ?
" My wife is young, handsome, and coquettish ;
" is that any miracle ? I have no doubt but she is
" a very good kind of a woman in her heart, but,
" were she not quite so much so as she is, justice
" should take place. Hitherto I have received no-
" thing but applauses from my friends : nothing
" can be more natural than my proceedings in this
" affair, and yet every body praises me, as though
" it contained something wonderful ! For my part,
" I imagine they did not give me credit for that
" much good sense.

" Pray how does the Marchionefs ? said Madame
" du Troëne, (the mother of Emily) purposely to
" change the subject of conversation.

" I warrant, continued Verglan, thou wilt some
" time or another become fond of her again.

" Faith, I think that probable enough.——It
" was but yesterday, after dinner, I detected myself
" saying civil things to her."

Really, interrupted Luzincourt, this is incredible.

Tell me, said the Viscount, have you ever heard
any thing like it in this house ?

Never ! This sort of effrontery is beyond all
bounds of probability.

Recollect too, that this passes in the presence of
an unmarried young lady, and a mother of most

excellent moral.——All this does not open the
eyes of Emily: " her heart excufes, in Verglan,
" the error of falling into the manners of the age."
She goes with her mother to the Theatre, the
play is *Ines & Nanine*. Belzor melts into tears,
Verglan laughs at his fenfibility. As they go
out, they meet with a Chevalier Dolcet in deep
mourning: he is left heir to an *old Uncle*, and
Verglan *gives him joy* of his ten thoufand crowns a
year; unwilling to let flip fo favourable an opportunity of fhewing the badnefs of his heart, and
bafenefs of his principles. Emily is ftill a witnefs,
and ftill in love. In the evening fhe looks on at
a party of Trictrac; Verglan is the worft of bad
players; Belzor has all the eafe and generofity
poffible; Emily fighs and fays, " I admire the one,
" but I love the other."

On the morrow Madame de Troëne was walking in the Tuilleries with her daughter, where fhe
found Verglan, with whom fhe entered into converfation. Let us read the paffage.

" The beauteous Nymphs, who, by their charms
" and accomplifhments, attract the young Defires
" who follow their foot-fteps, were affembled
" in the grand walk. Verglan knew them all,
" and fmiled as he caft his eyes around. Yonder,
" faid he, is Fatima, how paffionate fhe is! how
" affectionate! She lives perfectly well with
Cleon;

" Cleon; he has given her twenty thousand
" crowns within these six months, and they love
" like two turtles.——Look, this is the cele-
" brated Corinna, her house is the Temple of
" Luxury; not a woman in Paris gives such
" elegant suppers, and she does the honours of
" her table with the most enchanting grace.——
" Do you see the blue-eyed girl that has just
" passed us? Observe her modest air.——She
" has three lovers.——Her career will be brilliant,
" as I have told her.

" You are one of her confidants then, said
" Madame du Troëne?

" O yes: they know me, they are very sure
" they cannot impose upon me, and therefore
" never attempt to dissemble."

How is it possible to suppose, said Luzincourt,
that a man could carry on a conversation like this,
in the presence of a young lady he is going to
marry?

Ay, or in the presence of any well-bred woman
of fifty; yet Madame du Troëne takes Verglan
home to supper. In the evening she receives a
visit from a young widow, who speaks in a most
affecting manner of the virtues of her late husband.
Verglan ridicules her grief, and advises her to
take a handsome fellow. Emily at last overcomes
her inclination for Verglan, and marries Belzor.

H 2   And

And this, faid Luzincourt, is what is called, in the country, a picture of life and manners; this too is the reafon we find, in large country towns, fo many young men who affect the airs of Verglan, thinking they imitate a man of fafhion; a man who has undone fo many fine women. They imagine they fhall be very dangerous fellows if they can but imitate fuch extravagancies, and become fufficiently corrupt in their morals.

Add to which, returned the Vifcount, when a young man, thus fpoilt, comes to Paris, and is introduced into good company, he is fo ill received, and fo totally out of his element, that he cannot remain there long; he feeks other Society, where he finds himfelf more fupportable, and there he fixes. Thus a fool, by reading works like thefe, becomes the imitator of a rafcal upon fyftem; and thus weak people, who are eafily feduced, lofe, in part, their good principles, by imagining they may give way to their paffions, and openly defpifes law, decency, and good morals with impunity; and thus, laftly, the virtuous and feeling mind, by adopting this error, will deteft and fly the world; and, though formed for fociety, will become a morofe Mifanthrope.

Authors, who thus, through ignorance, have calumniated mankind, muft have made themfelves many enemies.

Not

Not in the leaft, no one acknowledges the portraits they have drawn; no one is hurt by them. Fenelon painted the Court, his picture was faithful, his likeneffes exact, allufions were imagined, applications made, and the Author of Telemachus was hated.

To return to the Moral Tales: you fee how neceffary it is to undeceive thofe, who imagine they contain a picture of our manners.

The work which fhould correct this miftake, would certainly be very ufeful (a). A man of fafhion only could be capable of the tafk.

If ever I write, I fhall fuppofe it my duty; it will be exceedingly painful to me to find fault with fo eftimable an Author, but I fhall dare to fpeak thus to him : I write for the benefit of youth, muft I leave them in fo dangerous an error ? I feel your abilities infinitely fuperior to mine, but permit me to fay, I know the manners of the polite world better than you.——The Moral Tales, however, have been written thefe twenty years, the Author

(a) And the more fo, becaufe Foreigners judge of the French from thefe Pictures, which give them the moft falfe and injurious ideas of our morals and opinions; the Englifh only treat us fo ill, in the greateft part of their works, becaufe they copy French Authors; and it is for this reafon they reprefent the French Fops in fo ridiculous and extravagant a manner.

has

has gained experience, and might eafily correct, in a new edition, thefe defects, and render a work totally good, which is fo very excellent in many of its parts.

As the Vifcount ended, every body returned to the Saloon, and the converfation became general.

The Vifcount, defirous of forming a ftricter intimacy with Luzincourt, invited him to his houfe. A mutual confidence was foon eftablifhed. Luzincourt informed the Vifcount of his projects, and read him fome Manufcripts, and the Vifcount confeffed to Luzincourt he was not happy. This avowal made the latter melancholy.——I do not deferve your pity, faid the Vifcount; I poffefs all the advantages man could wifh, but, by a fatal caprice, cannot enjoy them. I am frequently difcontented, idle, weary of myfelf, of every thing; yet I have a feeling heart, a family and friends, I love the beft of mothers, an amiable and virtuous brother, and a charming fifter-in-law. The truth is, I am in love, ferioufly and really, and have been thefe five years.

Is it poffible! cried Luzincourt, that Madame d'Herblay could infpire——

Is it poffible, interrupted the Vifcount, fmiling, you could imagine I alluded to her?

If

If not, how can you reconcile your attentions to her to your love for another?

Do you suppose love excludes gallantry?

Undoubtedly.

Look there now!——You believe in what has no existence among people of fashion.

Then people of fashion do not love.

The conversation was interrupted by the arrival of a visiter.

The Viscount introduced Luzincourt at the houses of his mother and his brother, where he was received with every civility and respect; his mildness, reserve, and the agreeable simplicity of his conversation, procured him, here, the same success which Damoville enjoyed in his own Society; he was soon admitted as one of the family, and treated as a friend of the house.

The thing which first struck him, was the remarkable change in the manners of the Viscount, especially to the ladies. Luzincourt no longer knew, in the gentle, the attentive, and the respectful behaviour of the Viscount, when at the house of his sister the Countess de Valrive, the man he had thought so full of levity, so satirical and unguarded, at Madame de Surval's. Madame de Valrive received company, almost every evening, from six till ten. A delicate state of health kept her at home, but she loved society,

· H 4   was

was amiable, and in vogue, and had a numerous acquaintance.

Luzincourt listened and observed in silence, and went, every morning, to acquaint the Viscount with what he had observed on the overnight. Hitherto, said he, I am enchanted with all I have seen; what a difference, between the people here and at Madame de Surval's! The visiters of Madame de Valrive seem to me all amiable, obliging, and witty; their conversations are generally trifling, yet have a charm which I know not how to describe; each speaks with ease and grace, and gives the most common compliments an agreeable turn. When conversation becomes particular, I do not find it instructive; it wants solidity, perhaps, but what gentleness! What decency! What respect in the eyes of each! And what a happy choice of words! Discussion never degenerates into dispute; self-love never takes offence, is never seen, except by it's desire to please; it is discovered only by it's attractions; it seems capable of being flattered and satisfied, but not of being wounded.

Hence said the Viscount, smiling, every body seems to possess wit, but cite me an example.

I own I cannot, replied Luzincourt; all I hear pleases me; but when I would recollect what it is, I am surprized to find nothing remarkable.

Such

Such is the effect of good breeding; it is that which produces thefe feductive illufions. You have pronounced the panegyric, not of the perfonal merit of thofe you have feen, but of what is juftly called politenefs and elegance of manner. To poffefs fuch advantages, you muft have an obliging and delicate attention to all; muft carefully conceal and reprefs the emotions of vanity; muft never betray a meannefs of fentiment, or badnefs of heart; but muft always fhew the utmoft decency, mildnefs, complaifance, and referve, a tafte for innocent amufements, and a love of virtue. Such is the exterior abfolutely neceffary in good company. I am forry it fhould be fo often deceitful; but it is the beft eulogium on virtue, to find no perfon can be amiable, who does not affume her language and her form.

While Luzincourt thus obferved the world, and communicated to his new friend his reflections and remarks, Damoville continued to divide his time between the Society of Madame de Surval, and that of the Men of Letters, by whom he was protected.

Luzincourt, however, defirous he fhould better know the world, obtained permiffion to prefent him to Madame de Valrive; where Damoville, defirous of fhining, fpoke a great deal; and as his defects were eafily feen, he was but coldly received. He told

Luzincourt,

Luzincourt, that Madame de Valrive was infipid and prudifh; that her vifiters were all deficient in underftanding; and determined, in fpite of the exhortations and advice of Luzinzourt, never to return to fo dull a houfe.

Damoville, a few days after, invited Luzincourt to a dinner he gave, to eight or ten of the Literati. They talked a deal, and did not rife from table till five o'clock, then all took leave of Damoville. As foon as Luzincourt and Damoville were alone, the former was afked how he liked the converfation.

You began, anfwered Luzincourt, by reciprocally praifing one another; you afterwards proceeded to your enemies, on whom you had little mercy; then followed differtations, citations, and difputations; but you did not converfe; each fpoke for himfelf, and pronounced his own ideas without troubling himfelf about thofe of others; you neither knew, attended to, nor fhewed each others abilities; you were either abfent or impatient when not fpeaking; you only thought of what you fhould fay next, and heard not half of what another faid to you: if any one told a good ftory, you could not enjoy it, becaufe you were bufy in endeavouring to recollect another; and you feemed affembled but to furpafs or fufpect each other, and not to amufe or inftruct: you all had one whimfical

fical kind of madnefs, which was to give the converfation fuch a turn as might introduce a joke,
or a bon mot, which you had by rote. Moft of
thefe bon mots, too, were to the glory of Men of
Letters, or Anecdotes concerning Men of Letters, for you thought only of yourfelves. Thefe
fhort quotations, thus multiplied, became weari-
fome, and thofe who liftened feldom enjoyed the
fatisfaction of him who related; neither do they
contain much inftruction, but made your converfation refemble thofe infipid books which are
filled with Anecdotes and Repartees, compiled
without care, and collected without a choice;
which may amufe for a moment, but which it is
impoffible to read through; and in which there is
nothing agreeable or witty that every body does not
know.

The remarks of Luzincourt did not vex Damoville; not yet become an Author, Damoville confidered him as a perfon of no confequence: his
franknefs amufed him, and he laughed at what he
called his frigidity.

Luzincourt continued with the fame affiduity to
vifit Madame de Valrive; the latter having great
confidence in Luzincourt, gave him to underftand,
fhe was not happy, though fhe had a confiderable
fortune, an amiable and good hufband, relations
whom fhe loved, and children that were her delight.

H 6   But

But her health was bad; the diversions of the town were no longer amusing; visiters fatigued her; she was weary of home; and she had neither the power nor desire to go abroad.

Alarmed at the languid state in which he saw her, Luzincourt secretly interrogated her Physician.—Madame de Valrive is at a *crisis*, said the latter, and she may continue thus for some time.

Of what kind?

I will inform you. The ladies of Paris have fallen into a set of habits, especially within these fifteen years, which naturally produce all the complaints of Madame de Valrive. Balls, *Traineaus* (*a*), and Tea, have destroyed a prodigious number.

But dancing is as healthy as it is agreeable.

Yes, when used with moderation; excess of any thing is pernicious. And however healthy it may be to dance in the open air on a village-green, it is far otherwise to dance all night, in a suffocating Ball-room, by candle-light.

But what fault do you find with taking an airing in a *Traineau?*

I affirm, this exercise can only be healthy to those who pass the winter at their country-seats.

And why so, Sir?

Because

(*a*) *A kind of winter carriage like a sledge, in imitation of a diversion very common in Russia, and the North.* *T.*

Becaufe they are accuftomed to the impreffions of the open air; they go abroad on foot, while the ladies here are continually fhut up either in their chambers, their clofe carriages, or their ftill clofer boxes at the Opera, to which cold air is inacceffible. Befides, if they rode out in their *Traineau* in the country, they would not go for mere parade, and in parties, which a fevere fenfation of cold would not permit them to break up. Here, on the contrary, if a young lady has once entered the cavalcade, fhe cannot think of quitting it, becaufe fhe feels herfelf getting cold, or finds fymptoms of a fore throat. Nothing can ftop her, away fhe goes, and returns ferioufly ill of a cold, which fhe will neglect in favour of a new party. Her lungs are next attacked, and fhe facrifices her life to the pleafure of being dragged up and down the ftreets of Paris, dying with cold, the tears in her eyes, her cheeks blue, her nofe red, her body crippled, her ears ftunned with the difcordant jingle of a thoufand bells, and converfing with her fellow traveller, on whom fhe turns her back, and by whom fhe can fcarcely be heard.

As to Tea, it is generally acknowledged, that the continual ufe of it is very dangerous; yet ladies live chiefly on Tea, Coffee, Cream, Butter, and Cakes. Is it wonderful then the ftomach

fhould

should lose its powers, or the lungs and nerves become affected? Therefore it is that their youth and beauty are lost so soon.   At five or six and twenty their constitution declines, and numbers perish at that age; then, too, they leave off dancing, they cannot support the fatigue, nor sit up all night.   If the principles of life are exhausted they sink to the grave, if not, sleep and rest retrieve them.   This is the reason why twenty-six is so dangerous an epocha to the Parisian ladies.   Madame de Valrive is past it, she is thirty-six, and yet she is at a very critical period.

How does that happen?

Thirty-six is the age when thoughtless ladies become weary of all the pleasures the world can afford: disgust and lassitude produce idleness and vapours: they stay at home, and are miserable; for what can become of those who have no rational amusement, and hate reading? They declare themselves Valetudinarians; the Physician is sent for, to whom they speak of nothing but themselves, for this is the only pleasure that remains.   Therefore it is, that so many Physicians and Directors are seen to succeed the Lovers, who have fled.

At length, unable to shine, to attract, or interest the affections of others, they keep their rooms; part of the day is spent in solitude, and absolute idleness gives time to think.   This situa-

tion,

tion, fay they, cannot endure for ever, we muſt
ſooner or later be cured, and quit our couches.
What is to be done then? Operas, Balls, Viſits,
have no charms. They have even loſt the love of
dreſs; flowers and feathers are forbidden, and diamonds are out of faſhion. What muſt become of
them?

Some choice, however, muſt be made, and
three things naturally preſent themſelves to the
mind; the lady muſt become either a Wit, a
Gameſter, or a Philoſopher; how to chuſe is the
difficulty. Madame de Valrive is at this point, ſhe
heſitates, conſiders, is melancholy and very uneaſy
in her mind, nor can her health be eſtabliſhed till
ſhe determines.

With ſuch a kind of illneſs, it ſeems to me, Sir,
ſhe might do as well without the medicines you ſo
continually order her to take.

What am I to do? I have told her ſhe is not ill,
ſhe perſiſts in affirming ſhe is dying; I muſt not
contradict her beyond a certain degree.

Why do you not quit her?

That would be worſe ſtill; ſhe would go and
be electrified, or take ſome other whim equally
dangerous. There is nothing which an idle woman, weary of every thing, bitterly regretting her
youth and beauty, and deſirous that the world
ſhould buſy itſelf about her, is not capable of doing.

ing. Formerly women had a thoufand trifling and innocent ways of drawing attention; they were afraid of Spiders, fcreamed at a Moufe, and fhuddered at the fight of two crofs knives; but fuch follies are out of fafhion. Philofophy will no longer permit fuch foibles, fuch childifh fuperftitions; knowledge is extended, and fuch tricks rejected; faintings and convulfions have fucceeded to thefe wretched arts; and people, pretending to be enlightened by fcience, difdain the fimple remedies of ancient Pharmacy: knowing the utmoft extent of the properties and virtues of the Loadftone and Electricity, they will not, as you may well fuppofe, undergo the reftraints of regimen, or drink calves jelly.

Luzincourt could make no anfwer to fuch reafons; he found the Doctor did not want fenfe, and was not amazed at his knowledge of women; he naturally acquired it by the duties of his profeffion. Men never fend for Phyficians but when they are really ill. Women always want their advice when they are idle or ill-humoured, and that is generally above half their lives.

Thus inftructed, Luzincourt profited by the confidence which Madame de Valrive repofed in him, to give her fome falutary advice; but he found at laft, fhe was abfolutely deficient in underftanding; that grace and eafe, which a knowledge of the world had given, had fo far feduced Luzincourt,

that

that he had believed Madame de Vairive equally witty and amiable. He learnt, with furprize, fhe was void of religious principles; fhe confeffed as much, or, to fpeak more properly, vaunted of it; he faw fhe intended, by this confeffion, to give him a high idea of the ftrength of her mind, and fhe cited the works which, as fhe faid, had delivered her from the prejudices of her youth. May I dare to afk madam, replied Luzincourt, if you are more happy at prefent?

Such prejudices are very inconvenient.

But are you not fubject to the fame decorum?

Undoubtedly that muft be fcrupuloufly obferved, becaufe of the confequences.

Therefore you fulfill all the exterior duties of religion?

Thefe may not be difpenfed with, efpecially as I am the mother of a family.

Yet believe none of them!——How tired you muft be of them!

You cannot imagine how much.

If you were not a *Philofopher*, you would obferve with zeal and pleafure thefe fame duties, which are now fo painful. What then do you gain by rejecting prejudices, as you were pleafed to call them? Since decorums muft be obferved, it is now that you are truly a flave, for your actions and conduct have no alliance with your fentiments.

You

You are right; and one is really often very much to be pitied, for having more knowledge than other people.

Are you certain, madam, of knowing the truth?

I have cited the works I have read.

You have no doubt read the refutations to thefe works.

Why fhould I? I am convinced; that is enough.

It feems to me, that the importance of the thing requires we fhould maturely weigh our opinions; for, where there is a doubt, reafons for, as well as againft, fhould be heard in the argument. What if it were proved, that the works, by which you have been feduced, were full of falfe citations; that their Authors knew not the holy writings they attacked; that their profound ignorance in that refpect was much like their duplicity, and that they contradict themfelves in every page?

You could not prove all that to me without tiring me to death; befides, I tell you once more, I am convinced; nothing can make me change my opinion: intolerance is repugnant both to the heart and underftanding.

You have heard long declamations on intolerance; but if you wifh to know what has been moft powerfully, moft feelingly, moft fublimely faid on that fubject, read the Gofpel.

All enthufiafts are intolerant, are perfecutors.

Enthufiafts,

Enthusiasts, like false Philosophers, are dangerous to religion; but the latter respect neither established order nor morality; yet I will not affirm philosophy is hateful and dangerous; nor should we calumniate religion and piety, because there are hypocrites.

But will not you allow it is impossible for a person of understanding to be devout!

Do not you believe that Nicole, Pascal, Racine, and Fenelon, had as much understanding as ourselves?

Yes; they had genius and understanding, but not Philosophy.

Do you think, madam, that Fenelon was absolutely without philosophy?

He had great talents——good intentions——but that is not what we mean by a Philosopher.

Certainly not a modern one. His works inspire virtue, of which his life was the most perfect model; equally great, in every station, favour or disgrace made no difference in his character and manners; he lived simple, benevolent, and disinterested, in the most brilliant Court of Europe; nor could persecution degrade or aggravate him; he had enemies, yet to him, Hatred was unknown; he was deceived, and Envy thought to triumph; but Fenelon gave addition to his fame, by condemning himself. Do you believe, Madam, your

Atheistical

Atheiſtical Philoſophers will ever afford us an example of ſuch ſublime Philoſophy?

You really amaze me. What! a man of your age, endeavouring to convert a woman! This is really ſomething new; but I muſt tell you I have ſome fortitude, and ſhall continue to maintain and defend my opinions.

You have not yet informed me, what your reaſons for theſe opinions are.

Reaſons! I have already given twenty; unanſwerable ones——but you know the Baron de Vercenay, who often comes here; it is impoſſible to have more wit. Well, Sir, he believes in nothing; abſolutely nothing; and were you to hear——

I am ſorry for him; but may I dare inform you, M. de Vercenay has very little knowledge.

You are deceived; no man of faſhion has more.

I ſuppoſed he had never read above four or five Authors in his life, and thoſe modern ones.

He has read every thing: aſk himſelf.

Your teſtimony is ſufficient.

He is an extraordinary man, and really deep; very deep.

Madame de Valrive rang her bell, her attendants came, ſhe went to her toilet, and Luzincourt retired.

In the evening he ſaw her Phyſician; I believe, ſaid

said he, your patient will foon come to a determination.

I will lay a wager fhe decides for wit.

I dare fay fo; but pray tell me how this can happen.

At prefent nothing is more eafy; formerly it was neceffary to find an entire new fet of acquaintances; the fafhionable world was totally abandoned, and men of letters only admitted; but now we have the happinefs to find a multitude of Authors in every ftation, and in every clafs. Madame de Valrive will invite, more particularly, thofe people of fafhion to her houfe, who pafs for perfons of wit. She will give them dinners three or four times a week; and in the evening will fay, fhe has fpent a charming day; will name every man who fat down to table, and affure her hearers, they never fhewed more wit or greater underftanding; fhe will praife the folidity of Chevalier de Sireuil, the graceful gaity of the Count de Morfan, and the originaiity of the Baron de Vercenay; not that fhe will have felt any thing of all this, but it is eafy to repeat what fhe has fo very often heard repeated.

She will then be obliged to attend thofe Authors who read their works in manufcript, and, inftead of a box at the Opera, fhe muft have one at the Playhoufe;

Playhouse; for she must never miss the first night of a new piece.

As she will not admit Men of Letters, no other works will be read at her house, but what are written by Men of Fashion.

Pardon me, Sir, a successful Man of Letters will always be well received, if he brings a Manuscript in his pocket; but, as soon as his work has been heard by all her acquaintance, her doors will be shut upon him, at least till he has written another.

And thus he is treated like a hired Singer, or instrumental Performer.

If Men of Letters were more conscious of the dignity of their profession, they would not have that kind of condescension for any but their particular friends, or those who desire to become such; for my part, were I to advise a young Author, I would tell him, Never be the dupe of your own vanity; never consent to act a subaltern part, to obtain the poor applauses of a few individuals: beware of pride, it debases whom it intoxicates, and sacrifices every thing to an inadequate and momentary success; it will render you absurd and inconsistent; will give you a dogmatic and positive air; will dictate the most ridiculous Prefaces, and yet, at the same time, make you eager to undergo the strangest humiliations.

Luzincourt

Luzincourt thought this advice very prudent, and resolved to profit by it.

While thus he lived, in the midst of new objects, Luzincourt, more sensible to the charms of friendship than even to the pleasures of observation and instruction, remarked, with chagrin, the Viscount came no longer to visit his sister-in-law. In vain did Luzincourt seek him, and above six weeks had passed away without his being able to see or meet him. At last, after a thousand fruitless attempts, he found him at home one evening. The Viscount received him as if they had only parted on the overnight: Luzincourt seemed melancholy, and the Viscount asked him the reason.

You promised me your friendship, said Luzincourt, and yet, for these two months, your door has been shut against me.

How could you suppose it? Every time you came I was either abroad or asleep.

Asleep! What at noon?

You forget dancing and gaming.

You love neither.

And yet I have done both.

Are you so altered then?

I well may be; but that is past; and I shall tell you some news that will give you pleasure. All is ended between me and Madame d'Herblay.

And have you no *ill* news for me?

None:

None : What do you mean?

Nay, I am not sent to question you, nor shall I dare indulge the least liberty of this kind, yet it is easy to see from your conduct——

I do not understand you ; speak plainly.

That there is some difference between you and your brother.

Not the least in the world, I assure you.

Then between you and Madame de Valrive ?

Neither: Who could tell you so improbable a tale ?

You do not go there any more ; at the beginning of the winter, you used to be there every day.

I once more tell you, dear Luzincourt, I have not for these two months past had a moment to myself.

And are you astonished not to find yourself happy? Live with your family and your friends, and you will then enjoy that pure content which alone can satisfy a heart like your's, and of which you have been robbed by dissipation.

You are right, I feel you are right ; and I am determined to reform habits of which I have been some time tired. It is now the spring, and if you will go with me, we will travel.

Luzincourt accepted this proposition with joy, and the Viscount, punctual to his promise, was ready to set off in the month of April. The two

friends

friends traverfed Holland, England, and Switzer-
land, and did not return to Paris again till the
middle of winter. Luzincourt, on his arrival,
learnt with joy that Damoville had gained the
Poetical Prize given by the French Academy.
Luzincourt read the verfes, and was then thoroughly convinced Damoville had known how to
gain friends, who had been more ferviceable and
zealous than juft. Damoville had a Medal; but
the Public, who have long fince learnt not to be
impofed upon by Prize Medals, found the Verfes
very bad; and fhocked at the partiality which they
faw take place on this occafion, forgot their ufual
indulgence to young Authors.

Damoville, encouraged by this triumph, was
confirmed in the opinion, that knowledge and
affiduity are ufelefs, and that to vifit and obtain
Patrons was the moft neceffary care. Six months
afterwards he publifhed a Novel, in which he
painted men and manners; that is to fay, fuch as
he had feen at Madame de Surval's. He told Luzincourt the work would create him many enemies.
I own, to thee, faid he, the portraits are drawn
after nature, a little overcharged, that they might
not be dull, but not the lefs like. My hero, for
example, is abfolutely taken from the Vifcount de
Valrive; I faw him only tranfiently at Madame
de Surval's, but I ftudied him minutely; I have

perfectly painted his mode of treating the ladies, his levity, his ironical and abfent air——

But I have before time told you, interrupted Luzincourt, this was all affectation.

My dear Luzincourt, you and I fee things in a very different light; befides, thy partiality for the Vifcount will not fuffer thee to fee him as he is; thou wilt give him talents to which he makes no pretenfion, and refufe him thofe agreeable qualities which have occafioned all his fuccefs with the women ; but I know him better than thou doft ; and hadft thou heard what Madame d'Herblay has told me of him !——Lovelace was a mere novice to him.

Canft thou give faith to the tales of a woman fo defpicable as Madame d'Herblay?

She is not more defpicable than others ; than Madame de Valrive, for example ; who, fince fhe was left by the Baron de Vercenay, has kept a little Opera finger.

Madame de Valrive?

Thou knoweft the fong that was made upon her.

What fong?

That which has been fo much in vogue.

I neither know the fong, nor this moft abominable ftory, which, certainly, never was heard out of the circle of Madame de Surval.

Not

Not in the circles thou frequenteft! But I tell thee, I am well acquainted with the intrigues of this town; the adventure of Madame de Champrofe; the double exchange of lovers between her and her female friend; the treaty figned before witneffes in the pleafure-houfe. Every one of thefe Anecdotes are in my Novel. Imagine then the confequence, and the noife it will make. Not but I have fomewhat difguifed facts.

I can affure thee there was no occafion; the Vifcount, Madame de Valrive, and Madame de Champrofe, have read thy Romance without the leaft emotion.

The effect of mere prudence; other people will be apt enough to make the applications, without their being fo filly as to betray themfelves.

I dare engage my life, thou mighteft write fuch works from this time till the day of thy death, without once moving their anger.

Luzincourt was right; but Damoville laughed. He vaunted of having written a Libel, becaufe he had committed to paper the fcandalous Anecdotes to which Madame d'Herblay had given breath; but thefe pretended Anecdotes were only abfurd calumnies, which nobody but her had ever heard of; neither were his portraits more faithful, for which reafon nobody took notice of it; nor did it make

I 2   the

the leaft *noife*; nobody, indeed, ever fufpected his malicious intentions.

Almoft all the Journals, however, affirmed, that fince the time of Crebillon, there had not appeared any work in which fo true a picture of men and manners could be found. This increafed the afto-nifhment of Luzincourt, who faw it was not pof-fible to attribute fuch exceffive praife entirely to the bad tafte of the Critics. Damoville, with his ufual indifcretion, informed him, how the fuffrages of certain Journalifts might be obtained; and the pre-fcription was, to get acquainted with fome of them, and give them little fugitive pieces for their Jour-nals; and as to the reft, Protectors and Friends would infure their good word.

Luzincourt objected, that this was very trou-blefome, tirefome, a great lofs of time, and could only obtain praifes by which nobody was deceived. Damoville replied, he knew the beft of all poffible extracts and praifes would produce no great effect in Paris; but that they were not ufelefs in the provincial towns, and foreign coun-tries.

Soon after this, Luzincourt made a journey to Champagne, where he ftaid two months with his father, and afterwards departed for Italy, which he was defirous of feeing, that he might one day

speak

speak of the arts, if not like a connoisseur, at least like a man of taste and understanding. An artist should live years at Rome; a few months are sufficient for a man of letters. The one must study, labour, and reflect profoundly; it is enough for the other to be struck, and to preserve the emotions and ideas of the sublime and beautiful. For this reason he ought to see St. Peter's, the Pantheon, the Apollo Belvidera, and all those other famous monuments, of which all the descriptions, designs, copies, and learned dissertations, that ever existed, can give but a faint idea.

After a six months tour, Luzincourt left Italy, and returned to Paris, where he accepted an apartment in the house of the Viscount de Valrive; who having for ever given up the fatiguing character of a man of the mode, led that kind of life which perfectly accorded with the disposition of Luzincourt.

While the latter was absent, Damoville had undertaken the Editorship of a Journal; and Luzincourt, shocked at several articles which had been sent him to Italy, could not forbear speaking of it to Damoville. Really, said he, your partiality is disgusting.

How so, prithee?

You praise works so intolerably dull——

Oh!

Oh! thou haſt thy eye upon the Pamplet written by Blimont; I allow it is deteſtable : but Blimont was ſtrongly recommended by a lady whom I muſt not diſoblige, I mean Madame d'Herblay; ſhe is at preſent miſtreſs to a great man, and has undertaken to ſolicit a penſion for me. She intereſts herſelf in behalf of this little Blimont; ſhe thinks him a man of wit and taſte ; and how could I avoid repeating this praiſe? Nay, I am well off to be ſo eaſily releaſed, for had ſhe by chance thought him a man of genius, I muſt have called him ſo.

Theſe are excellent reaſons. But then thoſe *Thoughts on various Subjects,* which were ſuch dull common-place ſtuff, and which you likewiſe ſo loudly praiſed, and thought ſo profound——

Them! Oh I might praiſe them without fear or reſtraint, very certain they would never be read ; nobody could contradict me, for I defy the moſt intrepid reader to go through three pages; therefore, when the Author is one of us, we boldly affirm ſuch a work to be ſublime. I formerly gave thee an example of this kind.

Yes, it is not thy fault if I am ſtill ignorant ; but though I might excuſe thy exceſſive complaiſance, who can excuſe thoſe bitter criticiſms, ſo full of gall, and ſo void of truth, againſt good Authors ?

How

How couldſt thou ſhew thy face, after thus praiſing Blimont, and thus abuſing Terval?

I own I have a great reſpect for the talents of Terval, and gave a very faithful and very advantageous account of his firſt work.

Well, but his ſecond is ſtill better.

Agreed; but not written in our principles.

What, becauſe he has affirmed religion to be the only ſolid baſis of virtue?

He has diſguſted all the Philoſophers.

Uſurpers you mean of this fine title.

Uſurpers be it; what matters it to me; he has created himſelf a multitude of enemies; and even if the moſt dangerous of theſe enemies had not been my protectors, I certainly ſhould not have been fool hardy enough to have aſſumed an ill-timed partiality. Aſſure yourſelf, Luzincourt, I am neither whimſical nor abſurd; and that I never praiſe a bad work or abuſe a good one, without ſufficient reaſon. Thus, for example, I gave a very bad character of the laſt new piece, and yet I thought it excellent.

And the Author has been one of thy friends above theſe ſix months.

This circumſtance makes my conduct ſublime; I ſacrificed him to gratitude. Laſt year the Editor of a certain Journal did as much for me, and one good turn deſerves another. He remind-

ed

ed me of the favour, told me the Author was his enemy, and I took that occasion to acquit myself of the debt. I did every thing in my power, to turn the Author and his piece into ridicule. Thou mayest tell me, likewise, perhaps, that formerly I was very loud in the praises of another Man of Letters, Dorgeval, whom I at present maintain to be a fool; but this is no caprice; we have quarreled beyond a possibility of reconciliation.

Who can answer reasons like these? And yet I must own, should I ever undertake the Editorship of a Journal, I should have a fancy to exhibit a model of the most perfect impartiality.

What a romantic! what an impossible project?

Not so romantic, since reason and personal interest would be sufficient motives. Nobody is deceived by the falshood of a Journalist, since the arts to conceal it have long been too common, and too well seen through. It is in vain, when they intend to abuse a work, they begin by affirming *they shall praise with pleasure, and find fault with regret.* In vain, when the Author is their friend, they inform us how *severe* they intend to be. We cannot any longer be duped by such shallow artifice; or, rather, after seeing such phrases at the beginning, we know what is to follow. Let me, therefore, advise you to change this old formula, and endea-

vour

vour to imagine something less known, and more likely to deceive.

Let us return to impartiality: I affirm it to be impossible, nay absurd. What if your intimate friend, or benefactor, had written a bad book; would you publicly proclaim it?

This is the only case, in which I should not think myself at liberty to speak my thoughts; but this does not often happen. And even when it did, I would not write against my conscience: were I obliged to make an extract from a work, under such circumstances, I should say, " The Book, which it " is my duty to announce to the Public, is written " by my intimate friend. I shall therefore confine " myself to the giving an idea of the plan, and mak- " ing an extract ; for, as my judgment might natu- " rally be suspected of partiality, I shall forbear to " give any."

And when you speak of your enemy, may not your judgment be as naturally suspected?

No. Friendship is all-powerful ; but my heart never can know hatred.

Persuade the Public to that.

I would prove it: the Public should be convinced I had at least understanding and greatness of mind sufficient to set my glory on being invariably equitable and sincere.

This

This is all very fine; but this *greatness of mind* would make thy Journal moft potently infipid.

Much lefs infipid than your's. You never fpeak candidly what you think; a thoufand narrow motives guide your pens, and when you praife the work, the reader fays, *How totally he is bought! How intimate he is with the Author!* And, on the contrary, when you criticize: *How he hates the Author! What an enemy he is to the Author! How much he fears the enemies of the Author!* And what dependence do you think fuch a reader will place in you? Such criticifms are read without emotion or curiofity; for, to know their purport, it is fufficient to know your prejudices, fears and antipathies. Inftead of which my Journal, without being better written, would indubitably be more amufing; the reader would be certain always of finding the true fentiments of an impartial perfon.

One would think thou wert fpeaking of a work defigned for the perufal of pofterity. Remember, a *Journal* is the thing in queftion; the mere thing of the day, which is often purchafed only to read the Play-bills; that is idly fkimmed over in the morning, burnt in the evening, and forgotten on the morrow.

Yes, fuch is the general fate of Journals; but is this the fault of the thing, or of the Writer? We have

have all heard how Addison, Pope, Steele, &c. amused themselves in writing these mere things of a day; the public had them in the morning, and read them at breakfast, and they were neither burnt nor forgotten on the morrow, but carefully preserved.

Oh yes; nobody will deny the Spectator to be an excellent work. The chief study of Authors formerly was to write well. They had not more wit than we have, but they had more industry. We want time : the life we lead neither admits of meditation nor labour.

I can easily conceive it is difficult enough to find time both for caballing and study.

For my part, I care little about this trifle of a Journal, the charge of which I have only taken for a moment. I shall soon quit it, and write one of a different kind, which will be much more serviceable to my affairs.

Of what nature ?

Not of a public one ; it will consist of a private correspondence with five or six foreign Princes, to whom I am recommended.

And what will you inform these Princes of ?

They are lovers of the French Literature, and desirous of knowing what new works appear before the Journalists publish their accounts. Thus I shall have an opportunity of sending the produc-

I 6

tions of all my friends; as to others, I shall content myself with an extract, and an *impartial* opinion, as thou sayest.

That is, when you dislike the Author, you will persuade the Prince the work is not worth reading.

Which he will surely believe from the extract I shall send.

The Prince will certainly be an excellent judge of the state of French Literature, and the merit of our writers, if he confides in thee.

I am not to be his Preceptor, but his Correspondent, and I care little about the goodness of his judgment.

And what advantages do you expect?

First, the pleasure of serving my friends, of establishing and increasing their reputation in foreign countries——

And of injuring your enemies. What else?

Fame and distinction. Pensions, Portraits, flattering Letters, copies of which will be published in the public Journals, and even adroitly inserted in my own works.

But pray tell me, how are you so suddenly to obtain the correspondence of six foreign Princes?

Wit and genius are first necessary.

These are the requisites: but for the means.

First carefully cultivate the friendship of Ambassadors, who will then on the publication of a

new

new work, undertake to present their Sovereigns with a copy; to this the Author muft add a letter to the Prince, and be careful to obtain recommendations from men of letters, his friends, whofe reputation is eftablifhed. Thus for inftance Dalainval did me this favour in Germany and Ruffia.

Thus inftructed concerning preliminaries, return we to the correfpondence. How is it poffible you fhould undertake fuch an enterprize?

What do you mean? Why not?

What! Clandeftinely rob men of reputation! Attack them without giving them the means of defence! Load them with accufations, and heap ridicule upon them, of which they are wholly ignorant! To which they cannot reply! Meet them continually, dine with them, fup with them, and part with them, intending to do them all the infidious mifchief in your power! Really, Damoville, I muft tell you plainly, there is fomething horrid in fuch conduct.

Thou art always in ftilts! Didft thou never, in a letter to a friend, indulge a fevere criticifm, or a hafty opinion?

Can you compare a letter to a friend, to a correfpondence like that you fpeak of?

According to thy principles it is horrid to write, unknowingly to the Author, that his work is bad.

I cer-

I certainly never fhould write fuch a thing but to a friend; and as I have no intereft to make them of my opinion, my criticifm would neither be captious nor long; it would be only a paffing reflection, not an endeavour to perfuade; and fhould my opinion be erroneous, I fhould hurt neither the Author's reputation nor fortune, therefore fhould only be guilty of rafhnefs.

Serioufly fpeaking, I acknowledge the correfpondence, I am about to undertake, demands the moft perfect equity.

But fuppofe yourfelf impartial, may you not be deceived, and unintentionally form a wrong judgment? Yes, Damoville, probity rejects clandeftine criticifms, they deferve to be claffed with libels. If you would attack others, prepare no fecret ambufcades, ftrike not in the dark, but face your foe, and avow your intention. Were I to write a criticifm, my motives fhould be juftifiable and moral. I fhould then combat, with fortitude, againft whatever offended reafon and manners; and as I know myfelf fallible, fhould wifh to be refuted and informed. Were the reply fcurrilous, or fcandalous, I fhould be convinced folid arguments were wanting; and, certain of being in the right, moderation would coft me little.

Suppofe you were proved in the wrong!

I would

I would inftantly own it; for, not having been wilfully fo, fuch a confeffion would fit eafy on my heart.

Pfhaw! If ever you fhould become an Author you will change your opinion, and your language.

Damoville pronounced thefe words in an ironical and half angry tone, rofe haftily, and took his leave; and as Luzincourt heard no more of him for upwards of two months, he fuppofed there was an end of all intercourfe between them. Damoville, however, though he thought Luzincourt odd and apt to cavil, could not forbear to efteem him, and depend upon his friendfhip. Habit and confidence made the converfation of Luzincourt neceffary. Determined not to follow his advice, he yet could not forbear afking it, and informing him of his hopes and fears. He would leave him in an ill-humour, yet muft return; and after neglecting him awhile, would again fuddenly come to inform him of his projects and fecrets.

Luzincourt in the mean time, continued the plan he firft laid down on his arrival in Paris. He fpent five or fix hours a day in company, and devoted the reft to ftudy, and what he held to be his duties. He never had neglected Darnay, the Advocate with whom he lodged the two firft years of his coming to town, nor broken the ftrict in-

timacy

timacy he had contracted with several eminent
Artifts. Simple, modeft, and natural, his manners were mild and noble, and his converfation
interefting; the women thought him pleafing, the
men wife, and his friends amiable.

Affectionate, and, confequently, benevolent,
he often vifited thofe obfcure corners where Mifery prefents her dreary afpect; and while he beheld all her woes, his heart acquired new fenfations. Compaffion became a principle! Compaffion, which dwells in all bofoms, though it
often lies latent, unawakened, unexcited by pathetic fcenes of wretchednefs! Like as fire is re-
fident in all bodies, even in flint, yet remains unknown unlefs forced into action.

At laft, faid Luzincourt, I now may write, I
now may affect the paffions without artifice. I
have feen fuffering Nature; I have beheld the
powers of Grief, Gratitude, and Magnanimity.
The cry of Defpair has rung in my ear! Terror!
Horror! Pity! Admiration! I have felt them all,
and I know the human heart. I have need neither
of Genius nor Imagination to paint with truth:
faithfully to remember what I have feen, heard,
and experienced, is all I want.

Accordingly he wrote and publifhed a moral
work, the fuccefs of which furpafled his hopes;
the paffions were moved, and Nature and Truth
were

were confpicuous.   Having no reputation, Luzincourt had no enemies, he therefore obtained univerfal applaufe : even the Literati loaded him with
praife.   Several of them came to vifit him and
gain his acquaintance, but after founding his inclinations they foon difcovered his principles, and
their enthufiafm began to cool.

Luzincourt perceived the tide turning, yet took
no ftep to overthrow the little confpiracy which
he found forming againft him ; they were angry
with themfelves, for having too indifcreetly praifed
a man who had an obftinate averfion to all party
fpirit ; but the fault was committed, and, while
they fought how to repair it, Luzincourt peaceably
enjoyed the fatisfaction of having given the world
a ufeful work, and the pleafure of feeing it tranfla-
ted into all the living languages of Europe.

Much about this time, Luzincourt became acquainted with a young widow named Aurelia,
who was vifited by many men of letters, and on
whom Damoville had paid conftant attendance for
the laft five months.   Aurelia was the widow
of a rich Merchant of Nantes, had no children,
and, finding herfelf at four and twenty her own
miftrefs, and poffeffed of a good fortune, returned
to live at Paris, with an old Aunt, who had brought
her up, and to whom fhe was fole heirefs.

                                    Aurelia

Aurelia had a handſome perſon, a cultivated underſtanding, a delicate taſte, a feeling heart, and a noble mind. She did not want penetration, but having too lively a fancy, ſhe did not always judge rightly ; ſhe was very liable to be prejudiced, but her prejudices were of ſhort duration ; ſhe loved truth, was ſincere in the ſearch of it, and had neither that obſtinacy which reſiſts its impreſſions, nor that ſtupid pride which rejects its conviction. She was often known to change her opinion; ſhe was accuſed of inconſiſtency and caprice, but unjuſtly, ſhe was only undeceived.

Naturally juſt and generous, no one knew better how to own, or how to repair an error ; her heart, formed only for friendſhip, was inacceſſible to hatred, envy, or reſentment. The firſt emotion over, ſhe not only eaſily pardoned ill uſage, but naturally forgot it. In ſpite of experience, ſhe was born to believe, as long as ſhe lived, in the ſincerity of reconciliations, and the impoſſibility of people continuing to hate each other.

Void of all affectation, incapable of hypocriſy and conſtraint, ſhe was not always equally amiable and prudent ; ſhe diſcovered too much indifference for thoſe ſhe did not think worthy her notice, and too much partiality for thoſe who pleaſed her. Wit and underſtanding may eaſily be deceived for a moment ; and Aurelia was always

ways

ways difpofed to believe Virtue and a fpecious behaviour were the fame. Good breeding is feductive, and adds an inexpreffible charm to the fenfations which admiration excites.

An illufion fo agreeable was neceffary to Aurelia, who could tafte no pleafures in which the heart had no fhare; fhe could be pleafed only by being interefted; and fhe too eafily attributed wifdom to thofe who appeared amiable. Her behaviour was gentle and equal; fhe did not make trifles important, took no light offence, claimed no extraordinary attention, but had defects and virtues feldom united in the fame perfon, and which gave her a certain fingularity equally original and inviting.

Communicative to excefs, fhe eafily betrayed her thoughts, but fhe fpoke only of her own concerns; friendfhip never had caufe to reproach her of the leaft indifcretion. She was giddy and imprudent, but not filly; fhe poffeffed fortitude, could fubmit to neceffity, fupport ill fortune, and keep a refolution; but it was only on great occafions fhe difcovered a great mind. In the common courfe of things, her complaifance fometimes looked like weaknefs.

Her natural activity, which was remarkable, was ufually exerted on ufeful and important objects; for when it was neceffary her mind was

firm

firm and determined. In indifferent things, she
was led and governed with as much ease as docility,
for she had an inexhaustible fund of gentleness and
good humour.

What, however, distinguished her most, was
the delicacy and nobleness of her sentiments; she
despised pomp and riches, contemned parties
and cabals. With an imagination less lively,
and feelings less quick, she would have had philosophy and superiority of reason; but she ceded
too soon to first impressions; more eager to be
informed, than occupied by the important care of
correcting herself, she gained knowledge, but not
perfection; she remained such as Nature had
formed her; and though she had not a common
mind, she had the defects of one.

Luzincourt was received at her house politely,
but coldly; she did not however forget to mention his work, but, with the most unaffected since-
rity, gave it the highest praise. Damoville soon
entered, and took the whole conversation upon
himself; Aurelia seemed to listen with great attention; Luzincourt observed it, and saw that
two or three of Damoville's friends, who were
present, took every opportunity to give consequence to all he uttered.

Damoville, on the other hand, was not pleased
to meet Luzincourt in this place. The latter
durst

durst not make his first visit so long as he wished, but renewed it in two or three days time. He was received the second time more coldly than the first; and when he departed, he went and supped at Madame de Valrive's, where he carried absence of mind and uneasiness, and therefore retired before midnight.

Instead of going to bed, he walked above two hours about his chamber, thinking of Damoville and Aurelia. It is evident he is in love with her, said he, or least pretends to be; he has beset her with his most intimate friends, who easily persuade her he is a man of wit, understanding, and virtue; she loves men of literature, and their purpose may soon be effected.——Yet Damoville is incapable of a sincere attachment——I am certain he is influenced only by a desire of making a good match, and will deceive a Lady worthy of a better fate.——Yet wherefore am I thus interested?——I own, I am somewhat piqued he should come, so often, to confide his silly schemes to me, and never mention a project like this.——'Tis strange! I long have known him as he is—— have no dependence on his friendship——and yet his want of confidence, in this instance, vexes me!

Internally

Internally difpleafed with himfelf, Luzincourt felt an infurmountable difcontent he had never known before. Damoville came to fee him next morning, and he bluflied and experienced a dif-agreeable emotion. Neither was Damoville to-tally free from embarraffment; but he foon re-covered his ufual appearance, and fpoke much, yet never mentioned the name of Aurelia.———— Thou wilt fee a letter of mine, faid he, to-mor-row in the *Mercure de France*, on Mufic.

Mufic! What have you to fay about Mufic?

What! A great deal about *Gluck* and *Piccini*.

But you never ftudied Mufic?

Writers at prefent muft touch on that fubjeet.

And fo you will write differtations on a fubjeet you do not underftand, confequently will write ill, will make falfe and ridiculous pretenfions to knowledge, and make two men angry with each other who were born for reciprocal admiration; and who, were it not for your trifling difputes, and the party janglings of inconfiderate zeal, would do each other juftice. Why, Sir, were even a Mufician, known to be fuch, a famous Compofer, to undertake a work, in which he fhould attempt to prove it is a folly to efteem the compofitions both of Gluck and Piccini, he would foon tire, but never convince his readers. In fpite of all the reafoning upon earth, thofe who

have

have fouls and ears will always love them both. Which way, then, can a Writer pretend to determine for a Nation, and fix its tafte, who does not underftand whether a Duet be made according to rule? How fhall he dare to fpeak in terms he does not know the meaning of, and imperioufly tell the world Gluck is a Barbarian, or Piccini has no Genius? This fpecies of madnefs is fo original it might amufe us, did it not give birth to anger and hatred; but your intolerance and animofity, make it as melancholy as it is unaccountable.

What is to be done? We muft fwim with the ftream, my friends are all Piccinifts.

I do not afk you to be a Gluckift, but you might be neuter.

What, and be hated by both parties!

If there be a thing on earth a true Philofopher can hate, it is certainly party fpirit; fince it gives birth to fuch extravagance, meannefs, and injuftice.

This letter was afked of me, it is written, and to-morrow it will appear. The die is caft, and I am now an avowed Piccinift for life. Should any one attempt to laugh at me, for not being a Mufician, I have a ready refource. I will imitate one of our antagonifts, who, hurt at this reproach, took a Mufic-Mafter at fifty, and began the

Violin-

Violincello. Thou mayeft fee I care little about my letter on Mufic, but thou wilt find in the fame Journal fomething more interefting: A Differtation on Englifh Literature.

Indeed! When did you learn Englifh? Three months fince you did not know a word of that language.

I have taken leffons fome time, and a few years hence may know fomething of the matter.

Being induftrious!—And in the mean time you will write on the fubject. This taftes of the *Violoncello!* You have no doubt made quotations in your differtation.

Many! I have cited Milton.

In Englifh?

Certainly.

But hark you, my friend! Who has corrected your proofs? You muft recur to the original for every word, for you will not perfuade me you underftand Englifh. I give you my word I will not betray you, tell me therefore how you manage, for the thing appears to me quite curious.

Curious! Not in the leaft; it is done every day.

What! To cite Englifh poetry, to reafon, to diffortate on its beauties, and defects, without knowing a word of Englifh!

Nothing

Nothing is more common: nor is any thing required for fuch a tafk, except a Dictionary, a copy of the original work, and a tranflation.

But thofe who underftand Englifh, will foon fee you do not.

Thofe who underftand Englifh, will not read our Differtations. It was abfolutely neceffary I fhould publifh thefe Fragments: a man of literature muft, at all events, appear perfectly to underftand a language fo univerfally ftudied at prefent, for the fake of his reputation in foreign parts, and the provincial towns. But, a-propos, I told thee fome time ago, **of a three act** Comedy I began laft **Spring**: it is finifhed, **and I** fhall read it to-morrow at Aurelia's. Wilt thou come?

Will —— will Aurelia —— permit me to be prefent? replied Luzincourt, fomewhat embarraffed.

O yes! yes! yes! I will take care of that.

Luzincourt hefitated a moment, and, after fome reflection, accepted the propofition.

Damoville could not forbear to tell him of a reading which **was** to take place **in** the prefence of thirty people, and which, to him, was a thing of the utmoft importance. On any other occafion, he would have been glad of Luzincourt's abfence; and he took fuch precautions on this, as quite robbed him of all uneafinefs.

Damoville had, in fact, formed a project to marry Aurelia; and, for this purpose, had introduced all his most zealous Partizans and Protectors, who, being privy to the intent, took every opportunity to second his design. Aurelia heard nothing but praises on the talents and virtues of Damoville; not a man, of the present age, had so well founded a reputation, was continually repeated in her ear. She knew he had borne away the prizes for Eloquence and Poetry, given by the French Academy, for two or three years; and they assured her, his celebrity was still greater in foreign countries.

Aurelia was not ignorant Damoville held a correspondence with several Princes, or that he received pensions, which she considered as honourable proofs of his superiority; his Panegyrists soon told all this, and how he had, already, been made a Member of the Provincial Academies; and that, they were well assured, he need but present himself, to be received one of the Forty of Paris.

So much lustre dazzled Aurelia. She was apt to think favourably of Genius; she loved Fame, and forgot there was nothing wanting to the renown of Damoville, but that of having deserved it. She examined not into causes, but was struck

with

with the effects; she enquired not, but was led. Besides, having never lived in the fashionable world, she was incapable of judging what were the merits of a work, which, she was told, was a perfect picture of high life. This picture, 'tis true, had somewhat offended her reason and natural good taste; but she heard so many voices raised in its praise, and contrary to her private opinion, for she durst not declare it, that she was obliged to accuse herself of an ill-founded delicacy.

Damoville was not deficient either in subtilty or suppleness; he saw Aurelia had noble sentiments, and a fixed aversion to party intrigues; and he spoke as though he possessed all the sublime qualities necessary to please a person of her disposition. Yet, though she thought him amiable, and supposed him a man of great abilities, she had not that heart-felt preference he flattered himself he could inspire. She admired him, however, and always shewed him a most decisive preference.

Such was the situation of Damoville, when Luzincourt first appeared at the house of Aurelia. Damoville knew of his introduction, and that Aurelia, the instant she had read his book, was very desirous of his acquaintance. Fearful he might become a dangerous Rival, Damoville neglected nothing that might injure him in Aurelia's opinion. It would have been too bare-

faced

faced to have openly fpoken againſt a man who
had been his firſt and moſt intimate friend; therefore, whenever ſhe mentioned his name, Dame-
ville took care to vaunt, with enthuſiaſm, of his
friendſhip for Luzincourt, but without ever praiſing
the friend or his works; he even hinted he had reafon to complain of him; but feigning to recollect
himſelf, as if he had done his friend wrong, he
ſeemed to reproach himſelf of indiſcretion, and
wiſhed to retract.

His Partizans need not ſpeak ſo cautiouſly: they
continually told Aurelia Damoville was infatuated
to Luzincourt, who, far from participating friendſhip ſo tender and ſo true, could not behold the
ſucceſs of Damoville, without the baſeſt envy;
that the latter had received the moſt outrageous
injuries from him; that he was an artful and profound hypocrite; and that, in fine, under an agreeable outſide, he concealed an unfeeling heart, and
a dangerous character.

Aurelia thus prejudiced, Damoville had little to
fear. He was defirous of being praiſed, eſpecially
in her preſence, and knew Luzincourt was no
flatterer; but then Aurelia would interpret his
ſilence into envy. It was this reflection that had
determined Damoville to invite him to the reading
of his piece.

. Though

Though Luzincourt was ignorant of thefe dark fnares, he well knew Damoville had acted with duplicity in this inftance. He felt how embar-raffing it muft be for him to hear a bad piece read, which his friend had written; but he fup-pofed, in a company of thirty people, he fhould neither be queftioned nor noticed. His defire to obferve Aurelia, during the reading, was great; and thinking he gave way to a mere emotion of curiofity, he went next day, at the time appointed, to Aurelia's.

Here he found a large company. Damoville was not yet arrived, and they, in the mean time, were bufy in his praife. Some of them who had heard the comedy read, affured Aurelia, it was a mafter-piece; they next vaunted his Letter on Mufic, and his Differtation on Milton, which Au-relia had read that very morning, and which fhe thought excellent.

Aurelia remarked, that Luzincourt liftened filently to his friend's praifes, and fhe was con-firmed in the opinion fhe had heard of his character. Of all the pangs the heart can endure, that of Envy is doubtlefs the moft infupportable; and yet it is the only one that cannot infpire pity: Aurelia, therefore, with an intention to augment the tor-ments of Luzincourt, praifed Damoville, even to exaggeration. Luzincourt was ignorant of her

K 3   projec,

project, and really supposed her desperately ena-
moured.   The idea made him melancholy; in spite
of himself, he was vexed, and fell into a gloomy
revery, in which he continued till the arrival of
Damoville, who was received by Aurelia in the
politest and most affable manner.

Damoville, before he began, endeavoured to
put his auditors into a favourable disposition.
Seven or eight people, in the company, guided the
judgments of the rest; to each of these he had
something agreeable to say ; one was assured, in his
ear, that his good opinion alone was the thing he
wished ; another was praised aloud for his taste and
natural indulgence.——After going round thus,
and making all these little necessary preparations,
Damoville gracefully sat himself down.

So well were his hearers disposed, that, as soon
as he took his work from his pocket, a confused
murmur of applause arose, occasioned by the
sight of this precious manuscript; every chair
was in motion to approach the reader, while
Aurelia, with a heart really interested, desired
silence.

Damoville, with a mild, modest, and insinu-
ating air, began, by reading an Advertisement,
which informed the assembly, that his little piece
had been sent to *Ferney*; that he had received a
most flattering letter, extracts from which he read ;

and

and that, finally, the suffrage of M. de Voltaire, and eight or ten other undoubted judges, had induced him to give his work to the public.

The Advertisement ended by a kind of analysis of his Comedy; that is to say, by a very circumstantial eulogium; whence it was clearly understood, that nothing so good had been written for these last twenty years; and that the Author had as much celebrity as genius. Several of them gave their thoughts on this Advertisement, which they pronounced equally modest and well written, and Damoville then began to read his Comedy.

He had before told them the wit of it was elegant, not gross, at which the understanding only could laugh. He did right, no one was inclined to laugh, though they all unanimously agreed, never had Author better seized the follies of the times; each exclaimed at every moment, How just! How severe! And those exclamations were so frequent, that an old Alderman of Toulouse, a relation of Aurelia's arrived overnight in Paris, cried out, as loudly as any of them, How just! how severe!

A witness of this universal enthusiasm, Luzincourt's embarrassment was increased, by perceiving Aurelia attentively observing him, and looking at him with indignation. He saw she thought him capable of that mean jealousy which Authors too often feel; the idea distracted him; for, in fact,

K 4

he

he was not at that moment free from jealousy, though it was of a very different nature to what Aurelia supposed.

He thought Damoville's piece intolerable ; however, to divert Aurelia's suspicions, he made an effort, and addressed some vague compliments to Damoville ; but as he was vexed with himself, and averse to the thing, he did this with so ill a grace, that every body took notice of his behaviour, every body began to whisper, every body's eyes were fixed upon him, and Aurelia gave him a look of contempt, accompanied with a disdainful smile, which compleated his confusion.

Damoville triumphed ; he observed all that passed, though, apparently, he observed nothing. The reading ended, he rose, approached Aurelia, and with the utmost seeming candour, said, Can you guess what I am thinking of ?——Of you, Madam, and Luzincourt.——I have the happiness to obtain your applause, and I have a friend, who knows my heart, who participates my joy ; a witness of this most pleasing, most flattering success.——Yes, I know he participates my joy.——He may have his failings, but have not I too ?——Who is without ? My delicacy is great, but I have often pushed it too far, especially with him——Yet I have always done his feelings justice——and even, at this moment, I am certain they are exquisite.

This

This apparent credulity of Damoville, affected Aurelia fo much, that fhe was obliged to turn her head afide, to hide her tears ; then looking at Damoville, with great expreffion faid to him, the thing I am moft certain of, is, you are worthy a fincere friend.

Worthy of one ! I have one ; at leaft, added he, fetching a deep figh, I flatter myfelf I have——— Even were it an illufion, it would be cruel to rob me of the agreeable fhadow.

Damoville pronounced thefe words with fo tragical an air, that Aurelia was greatly affected ; her emotion was vifible in her countenance ; and Luzincourt, though at the other end of the chamber, perfectly beheld her tendernefs and trouble. Then it was he indeed envied Damoville, and felt a pang of heart fo fevere, he could not hide what paffed in his mind, but rofe to take his leave.

Damoville called him back, and he returned with confufion in his face : Damoville had not quitted his chair, which ftood next to that of Aurelia——When, my friend, fhall I fee thee ? faid he.

This fimple queftion quite confounded Luzincourt, who anfwered, with a frozen coldnefs, he was very bufy at prefent, and——

K 5

He

He could not finish his sentence; for he neither knew what he said, nor what he wished to say.

I will call on thee to-morrow, said Damoville.

Do not give yourself that trouble; I shall not be at home.

But betimes, before thou art out.

Luzincourt, not knowing what to say, answered, he was going into the country for a few days; then turning towards Aurelia, asked if she had any commands; who, without deigning to look at him, replied by a simple inclination of the head; and Luzincourt, making a low bow, instantly left the room.

As soon as he was gone, Damoville, looking at Aurelia with an air of astonishment, exclaimed, I am quite petrified! What is the matter with him? ——This is inconceivable!——Have I said any thing to give him offence?——It is true, this is not the first time I have seen him so; but, I confess, I hardly know how to support such behaviour.

Aurelia, full of pity for Damoville, sighed, and changing the conversation to divert his thoughts, once more began to praise the charming piece she just had heard.

The unhappy Luzincourt ran to his real friend, the Viscount de Valrive, to tell him all that had passed. Never, said he, again will I enter that fatal house. I had heard so flattering an account

of

of this Aurelia, that I gave way to my defire of being acquainted with her. Before I ever faw her, I received feveral letters from her, all of which fpoke her a woman of wit and underftanding; but fhe is paffionately in love with Damoville, and it is impoffible fhe fhould have the leaft difcernment; never will I forgive myfelf the ridiculous fcene I have feen playing at her houfe; but I was vexed, and had loft all command of my temper; I——

And fo, my dear Luzincourt, interrupted the Vifcount, fmiling, thou art in love at laft.

I in love! How is it poffible I fhould love a perfon whofe heart is engaged, and who has made fo wrong a choice.

You flatter yourfelf this choice is not yet made; and, indeed, if her head and heart are good, fhe will foon be undeceived; vifit her often, and her prepoffeffions will foon vanifh.

It is not poffible I fhould longer look on Damoville as my friend. I foon found out his principles and fentiments, and yet I loved him. The remembrance of our former friendfhip impofes duties on me I never can forget; Aurelia fhall not learn his character from me.

Nor need fhe; let her do you juftice, and you are certain of obtaining a preference.

K 6

I hope

I hope at leaft, fhe will fome time know me incapable of odious vices. I own it it impoffible I fhould not wifh for her efteem——I will fee her once more, and if fhe really loves Damoville, I have the power to be filent; fhe never fhall know my thoughts.

Some days after this converfation, Luzincourt vifited Aurelia; he found her alone, and reading, with the tears running down her cheeks. Luzincourt perceived it, and was going to retire; Aurelia called him, and he returned. The book fhe had been reading lay open on her knees, and fhe was a moment filent. At laft, looking at Luzincourt, fhe faid, A work ought to be very excellent indeed, to move one fo much at a fecond reading. It is about a year fince this firft appeared, and I read it then; you now fee how much it affects me.

Luzincourt, perplexed, faid, with a trembling voice, the Author is very happy.

Happy indeed, replied Aurelia; if it be true, he painted his own mind in his work. So faying, fhe prefented the book to Luzincourt, who caft his eyes on a page moiftened with Aurelia's tears, and faw, with tranfport, it was his own writing.

Oh flattering eulogium! cried Luzincourt.

He

He durſt not proceed——Aurelia fixed her eyes upon him. After a few moments, he once more broke ſilence, and ſaid, Do you then, madam, believe it poſſible, an Author ſhould truly expreſs ſentiments he never felt?

I have always thought the contrary, and yet——

And yet what, madam?

Permit me to ſpeak freely.

I conjure you ſo to do.

You know how to paint the charms of friendſhip, in the moſt affecting manner: but do you know as well how to fulfil its duties?

You have deigned, madam, to ſpeak plainly; may I take the liberty to aſk what could have given birth to ſuch a doubt?

My own obſervations.

Pray heaven, madam, that, with an equitable mind, you may have ſeen only with our own eyes.

Well, ſince you wiſh me to ſpeak without diſguiſe, I muſt own I was greatly ſurprized at your behaviour, when you laſt were here.

I acknowledge, replied Luzincourt, ſmiling, appearances were againſt me; I felt they were, too forcibly; and it was this ſenſation alone, that made me ridiculous.

Luzincourt pronounced theſe few words in ſo calm, ſo natural a tone, that the moſt circum-
ſtantial

ftantial explanation could not have been more perfuafive. Aurelia, forcibly ftruck, beheld him with extreme furprize.   I cannot conquer my aftonifhment, faid fhe, you have not given me a fingle reafon, and yet I am convinced.

Such, madam, is the force of truth.

But why were you fo confufed then?

Unhappily for me, I difcovered you were pre-judiced againft me, and that you fufpected me of envying Damoville's fuccefs; I was chagrined, and this made me commit fo many aukward blunders.

I have wronged you, and I fhall never pardon myfelf.

Aurelia pronounced this fentence with fo fincere and graceful a candour, that Luzincourt, tranf-ported, was half tempted to throw himfelf at her feet; he reftrained himfelf, however, and con-cealed a part of his emotion.   Aurelia queftioned him further.   I confefs, faid fhe, I praifed your friend's piece, with a little exaggeration, but pray what do you think of it?

It feems to me at leaft as good as moft of the trifles in one act, and in three, which have been played within thefe fifteen years, and in which they have pretended to exhibit men and manners. I fhould prefer it, for inftance, to the *Circle*, or the *Feinte par Amour*: that over-refined fafhion-
                                            able

able Marquis, who seduces all the women, by shewing them how to embroider, make work-bags, and knit garters, is an imaginary Being that never had existence. Though trifles may some-times please the women, they certainly would not chuse a man who spent his time in knotting, knit-ting, and embroidering; such puerilities have only pleased on the stage, because a delightful Actor has given them graces which are purely his own, and because most of the spectators, being ignorant of life, believe this caricature to be a picture of it; but nobody reads these pieces, which they take a pleasure to see.

It is certain no piece can be good, which does not affect us by reading it; yet, do you suppose a bad piece may remain so long on the stage?

It certainly may remain as long as the Actor, who first gave it success.

The duration of our errors is short, in proportion to the length of our lives; we continually deceive ourselves, but we are as quickly undeceived; and, were it not for this happy facility, our mo-mentary and brittle being would exist only in a dream. But who shall dare hope to find the truth, if an illusion may endure fifteen years?

There does not seem to me any great illusion in this: an Actor, inimitable in his walk, is ap-plauded; nothing more. Generally speaking, the

Public

Public do juftice to Authors and their works; but let me remark, the Town is difficult, in proportion to the length of the piece; if it be in five acts, it muft be perfect; if in one, they care little how bad it is; and this is the reafon, why fo many fhort pieces, below mediocrity, and even below contempt, continue to be played.

Let us return to Damoville. I have only one doubt, which you may remove, for I feel you have gained my confidence. Tell me, if you verily believe you have as fincere a friendfhip for Damoville as he has for you?

I perceive, madam, you have much too extravagant an idea of Damoville's friendfhip for me; there is no great intimacy, at prefent, between us; we keep very different company, and fee each other feldom.

I know that, haftily interrupted Aurelia; but is it his fault or yours? He certainly confiders you as his deareft friend.

No, indeed, madam.

No!——Why?——

His deareft friends are thofe, who procured him the pleafure of your acquaintance.

Scarcely had Luzincourt fpoken the laft word before the door opened, and Damoville was announced. Aurelia blufhed—Luzincourt, no longer agitated by his former fears, did not difcover the
flighteft

flighteft emotion, while Damoville, in his turn, was fomewhat difconcerted. He foon, however, recovered himfelf, and, according to his plan, began to load Luzincourt with profeffions of friendfhip, and reproached him for having faid he fhould go out of town, when he had no fuch intention.

It is true, faid Luzincourt, I had no fuch intention; I was guilty of deceit, and I did wrong. I fuffered for it; you know I am not fubject to fuch meannefs; neither am I apt to be out of temper; I own I was the other day, and I have been juft confeffing it to this lady; fhe was the innocent caufe of my weaknefs, and, in juftice, ought to receive the firft apology.

Luzincourt's franknefs and fincerity, furprized and embaraffed Aurelia. As for Damoville, he knew not what to think: his inquietude was exceffive. Luzincourt, unwilling to keep him long in pain, rofe and took leave of Aurelia; then turning to Damoville, Well remembered, faid he, I have a meffage for you; Madame de Valrive, and Madame de Champrofe, wifh much to hear your Comedy.

Oh, replied Damoville, I am teized to death on that head. I read it yefterday to the Dutchefs of —, and fhe has defired me to repeat it again

to-

to-morrow. People really have no mercy on good nature.

What answer shall I give the ladies?

I have refused Madame de Clary, who has perfecuted me beyond all belief; nay, I have positively this very morning, denied to go to the Princess of ——.

Am I to understand this as a denial?

To be sure; and let me entreat thee, my dear Luzincourt, not, in future, to undertake any such like messages.

After this final answer, Luzincourt bowed, retired, and left his Rival alone with Aurelia.

(1) IT is very certain there exits a method, by which a gentle and induftrious child may learn to read currently in fifteen leffons; and the dulleft will not need more than four months; while, according to the prefent method, eighteen months or two years will be neceffary. M. Berthaud has taught us, that eighty-eight combinations of the letters, will include all the founds; that is, he has difcovered, that all the words in the French language are included in thefe eighty-eight confonances; fo that thofe who know their formation (without thinking on the letters which compofe them) have learnt to read; and as he has applied a figure to each of thefe confonances, the child eafily remembers it, and learns to read in two months. This method cannot be here circumftantially explained, the work which teaches it muft therefore be referred to, the title of which is *Quadrille des Enfans, ou Syfième nouveau de lecture*. It is fold at Paris, chez Couturier, Quai des Auguftins.

The Editor of the laft edition of this work, is M. Alexandre; who is the only perfon that teaches by this method. He lives in the Rue Montmatre au coin de la rue Plâtrière.

It is very extraordinary this method has not yet been univerfally adopted, fince it has been invented near forty years;

years: but such is the attachment of men to an old track, however bad it may be.

(2) A French woman, *Elizabeth Sophie Chéron*, distinguished herself equally in Painting, Poetry, and Music. She played on several instruments, understood Latin, Italian, and Spanish; painted Portraits well, but always in some allegoric and ingenious manner; and has, besides, left several Historical Pictures. In the same year, she was made, in quality of Poet, an Academician of Ricovrati at Padua, and was received a Painter, in the *Académie Royale de Peinture & de Sculpture* of Paris. She married, when she was 60, her intimate friend, an Engineer, named M. Hay, who was of her own age, and died at 63, in 1711 (a).

Catherine Duchemin, the wife of *Girardon*, a Sculptor—*Geneviève* of Boulogne, and her sister, *Madeleine* of Boulogne, are three other French women, who particularly distinguished themselves in painting. But let us speak now of foreigners.

Anna di Rosa, surnamed Anella de Massina, from her Master, painted History with great success (b).

(a) Her most esteemed Historical Pictures are, 1. The Flight into Egypt, with a beautiful Landscape, where the Virgin is seen sleeping, and the Angels taking care of the child Jesus. 2. Cassandra interrogating a Genius, on the Destiny of Troy. 3. The Annunciation. 4. Christ at the Tomb. 5. St. Thomas Aquinas. She has left several agreeable Poems; one, among others, entitled Les Cerises renversés, or the Cherries overturned; in which are ease, gaiety, and imagination.

(b) She perished at 36, the victim of jealousy; being poniarded by Augustin Beltrano, her husband, who was hurried away by unjust suspicions.

Sophonisba

Sophonisba Angosciola Lomellina, of a noble family of Cremona, enjoyed and merited great reputation. Philip II. of Spain, invited her to Madrid, where he loaded her with favours, and procured her a most honourable match. Being become a widow, she took to her second husband, Orazio Lomellini, who was one of the most illustrious families in Genoa. She herself taught the principles of her art to her three sisters, Europa, Anna, and Lucia, who all painted with success. Sophonisba lived till she was exceedingly old, and died in 1620.

Lavinia Fontana, and *Antonia Pinelli*, of Bologna, deserve also a place among celebrated Painters.

Maria Elena Panzachia, born at Bologna, in 1668, painted landscapes in a superior style.

Lucia Cessalina, born in 1677, painted History and Portraits with equal success. She married Felix Torelli, one of the best Painters of his time.

Catherine Taraboti, the Scholar of Alexander Varotari, deserves a place among the best Artists of the Venetian School. The sister of Varotari, named Clara, painted Portraits in perfection.

Barbara Durini was born in 1700, and had abilities equal to any already cited.

The Flemish and Dutch Schools have produced women equally celebrated. The famous Sibylla Merian has been already mentioned. Anna Waffer was born at Zurich; she loved letters, wrote good poetry, painted agreeably in oil, but excelled in miniature. She died in 1713, aged 34.

Mademoiselle Verst was born at Antwerp in 1680; knew Latin, spoke several languages, and painted Portraits and History: the most celebrated Artists have agreed

in

in praising the freshness of her colouring, and the purity of her designs. She went to London, where she died.

Maria Van-Oefterwick is justly placed among the best Artists of Holland. She painted only fruits and flowers; but she painted them in the highest perfection. She died in 1693.

Henrietta Vanpea-Volters, her Father's Scholar, was born at Amsterdam, and was eminent as a Miniature Painter. She died in 1741.

Rachael Ruisch Van-Pool was born at Amsterdam, and was one of those women who most have honoured her country by her manners and talents. Young, without matter, without assistance, her taste for drawing led her to copy whatever struck her in paintings or engravings. At length, she was put under the tuition of William Van-Aclst, who was celebrated for his fruits and flowers; in which kind of painting she obtained the highest reputation. The Academy of the Hague received her as one of its members, as they also did Van-Pool her husband, who was a good painter. The Elector Palatine sent her a diploma, constituting her painter to the Court of Dussfeldorp. The Prince sent her a letter, accompanied with a magnificent present, and stood godfather to her child. She painted as well at eighty as at thirty, and died, aged eighty-six, in 1750.

The celebrated Van-Huopen excelled in the same style, and had only one scholar, the daughter of a person named Haverman, who made such an astonishing progress, as even to excite her master's jealousy.

Time has not destroyed the names of all the women of antiquity, who have distinguished themselves as Painters. The most celebrated are,

" Timaretta,

" *Timaretta*, the daughter of Micon, and who excel-
" led in the art.

" *Irene*, daughter and scholar of Cratinus.

" *Calypso*.

" *Alcisthene*.

" *Aristarete*, the scholar of her father Nearchus.

" *Lala*, of Cyzicus.   No person had a lighter touch ;
" she engraved also on ivory.

" *Olympia*, whom Pliny mentions."

> *Extraits des dif. Ouv. Pub. sur la Vie des Peint. Par*
> M. P. D. L. F. *Tome. I.*

I have collected, from the work above cited, various
other circumstances, little known, which appear to me
curious and interesting.   I have supposed they might
be read with pleasure, and perhaps excite emulation
in the minds of youth, who have a propensity to the fine
arts.

" *Polignotus*, the son of Agloophon, a celebrated Pain-
" ter among the ancients, lived about four hundred and
" forty years before Christ.   He was the first who gave
" expression to the countenance ; and after having paint-
" ed several pictures at Delphos, and under the porticoes
" of Athens, for which he would receive no payment,
" he was honoured by the Council of the Amphictiones,
" with the solemn thanks of all Greece, who decreed him
" apartments in all the cities at the public expence, or-
" dained him golden crowns, and assigned him an ho-
" nourable seat in the theatre.

" *Apollodorus*, an Athenian Painter, lived four hun-
" dred and four years before Christ ; opened a new ca-
" reer, and gave birth to the fine age of painting in
" Greece.   His talents were great ; but what was still

" more

" more to his honour, he was free from jealoufy, a weak-
" nefs too common among artifts. He wrote verfes in
" praife of Zeuxis, his rival, in which he owned himfelf
" inferior to that great man.

" *Pamphilus* acquired high reputation, even in the age
" of Parrhafius and Zeuxis. He was above other Pain-
" ters in thofe advantages, which the cultivation of the
" Belles Lettres and fcientific ftudies afford. To give
" his art the greater dignity, he obtained a public de-
" cree, which forbad the exercife of it to flaves.

" *Paufius*, the difciple of Pamphilus and Erigmus, was
" the firft who adorned palaces by painting their cielings.
" He immortalized the flower-girl, Glycera, with whom
" he was in love, by reprefenting her compofing a gar-
" land of flowers.

" *Metrodorus* was both a great Painter and a great Phi-
" lofopher. He educated the children of Paulus-Æmi-
" lius, and painted his triumph. This hero had de-
" manded two men to execute thefe two different tafks.
" Metrodorus was thought moft capable of fulfilling
" them both.

" *Quintus-Pedius*, a Roman Painter in the time of
" Auguftus, diftinguifhed himfelf in that art, though
" born dumb."

We fhall now pafs on to modern Painters.

" Painting began to be known in Florence about the
" year 1000. Some Greeks were brought from Conftan-
" tinople, to paint the choir of a church in Mofaic. The
" art, however, did not approach perfection till the year
" 1211, when John Cimabua was born. This artift
" performed feveral works, which banifhed the Gothic
" and barbarous tafte that fo had long degraded the fine
" arts.

" arts. Cimabua was alſo a good Architect : the protec-
" tion afforded him by Charles of Anjou, King of Naples,
" was one great means of the progreſs of the art. Cima-
" bua died in 1300.

" *Giotto* was the ſcholar of Cimabua ; his father, who
" was a Farmer, ſent him to keep his flocks. Giotto
" amuſed himſelf with painting them ; and Cimabua,
" who happened to paſs, and ſeeing him thus employed
" perſuaded him to go with him to Florence. Here
" Giotto ſoon equalled his maſter : among others, he
" painted the portrait of Dante : he painted landſcapes
" alſo, and cattle ; and died in 1336, at the height of
" honour and riches.

" *Anthony Solario*, ſurnamed Zingaro, a Lockſmith,
" fell in love with the daughter of Cola Antonio, who
" diſdaining his profeſſion, told him, he ſhould never
" marry his daughter till he was as good a Painter as
" himſelf. Solario travelled, ſtudied, and at laſt arrived
" at ſuch perfection, as to obtain the woman, for whoſe
" ſake he became a Painter. He was afterwards a good
" Architect, lived to the age of ſeventy-three, and died
" in 1455. He left many ſcholars, who became excellent
" Artiſts.

" *Andrew Verrochio* applied himſelf to Painting and
" Sculpture ; and inſtructed himſelf in the principles of
" Architecture, Perſpective, and Mathematics : to theſe
" he likewiſe added the arts of Engraving and Muſic.
" His ſchool was that in which the beſt Artiſts of his time
" were formed. Such were Peter Perugin, and Leonard
" de Vinci. Andrew Verrochio was the firſt who at-
" tempted, and ſucceeded, in caſting the faces of living

" and dead fubjects, to obtain their likeneffes. He died
" in 1483.

" *Guido Reni*, beft known by the name of Guido, was
" born at Bologna in 1575. He learnt the firft prin-
" ciples of painting from Denis Calvart, a good Flemifh
" Painter, and afterwards ftudied in the fchool of Louis
" Carracio. According to Guido, the eye was the moft
" difficult part of the countenance to paint, to which he
" therefore more ftudioufly applied, and more perfectly
" reprefented, than any other Artift. His fchool con-
" tained near two hundred ftudents. He died in
" 1641 (*a*).

" *Anthony Baleftra*, a great Painter of the Venetain
" School, died in 1740, aged feventy-four. What was
" moft fingular in him was, he did not attain perfection
" till he was old.

" *Giovanni-Francefco Barbieri*, furnamed Guerchin,
" or the Squinter, was born at Cento, near Bologna, in
" 1590. No Painter ever worked fafter than this great
" Artift. Preffed by fome Friars for a picture of God the
" Father, for the High Altar of their church, on the
" eve of their feaft, he painted it one night by candle-
" light. He died in 1666 (*b*)

" *Auguftin*

(*a*) Guido's beft painting is in Italy, at Bologna, in the Sam-
pierri Palace. The fubject is St. Peter in prifon, weeping for his
fin.

(*b*) There is a very ftriking picture of this mafter, at Capodi-
monte, near Naples. It is a half-length Magdalen, to which
common

" *Augustin Metelli* was born in great poverty, at Bo-
" logna, and at the age of seventeen had acquired so
" much perfection, that a rich Architect sought him out,
" and offered to divide his fortune with him, and adopt
" him for his son; which offer Metelli's love for his fa-
" ther and mother occasioned him to refuse. He after-
" wards went into Spain, where he received numerous
" favours from Philip IV. He was an excellent Archi-
" tect, a man of Literature, and wrote good Poetry.
" He died at Madrid in 1660.

" The Chevalier *Stanzioni*, a Neapolitan, became fa-
" mous in Painting and Architecture. He has written
" four books, full of useful reflections, with the lives of
" the Painters and Sculptors of his own country. He
" lived to the age of ninety-six, and died in 1681 (*a*).

common subject he has given novelty, by his manner of treating
it. His Magdalen does not express despair, but a sensation more
confirmed and profound. Her head is supported by her hand, in
which melancholy attitude she contemplates Christ's Crown of
Thorns, which lies before her on the table. To celestial beauty
her countenance adds expression, as affecting as it is sublime;
and represents, with perfect truth, all the reflections to which
such meditations might be supposed to give birth.

(*a*) Joseph Ribeira, surnamed the Little Spaniard, was born
in poverty, became very industrious, and acquired great perfection. A Cardinal took him to his own house, but the Spaniard finding himself too much at his ease, and observing his industry slacken, he fled from the Cardinal for that sole reason recovered his love of labour, and made a great fortune. He died
1746.

" *Juan*

" *Juan-Fernandes Ximenes de Navereta*, known by the
" furname of *el Mudo* (the Dumb) is called, by the
" greateft Artifts, the Spanifh Titian. He was celebrated
" by the moft famous Spanifh Poets, and died in Spain
" in 1572 (*a*).

THE FLEMISH, DUTCH, AND FRENCH SCHOOLS.

" *Louis de Deyfter*, born at Bruges, was a great Pain-
" ter, and an admirer of the Italian manner. He amufed
" himfelf with making harpfichords, organs, violins,
" and clocks. Anne Deyfter, his daughter, drew well,
" and made copies of her father's works, which have
" often been miftaken for the originals. She was like-
" wife a Muſician, played on all inftruments, and excel-
" lently on the harpfichord. Deyfter died in 1711.

" *Octavius Van-Veen*, a good Painter, died at Bruffels
" in 1634, and left two daughters, Gertrude and Cor-
" nelia, who both excelled in painting.

" *Gerard Terburg*, born in the province of Overyffel,
" an excellent Artift, died in 1681. Netſcher, Coutſon,
" and Koetz, were his difciples, and his fifters; Maria
" Terburg, his daughter, fketched out his works, which
" were as much efteemed as if they had been totally his
" own.

" *John Both*, born at Utrecht, furnamed Both of Italy,
" becaufe of his long ftay in that country with Andrew

(*a*) John Holbeen, furnamed the Young, a German, could
paint only with his left hand. The Dance of death, at Bafil, is
by him, and reprefents Death deftroying all human grandeur. I
have feen the picture; I found it impoffible to underftand its
beauties, but it is admired by all Connoiffeurs. Holbeen died
at London in 1554.

" Both

"Both, his brother, fucceeded fo well in imitating the
"colouring of Claude Lorrain, that the reputation of
"Claude was diminifhed; and the more fo, becaufe
"that the figures of Andrew Both, his brother, which
"were inferted in his landfcapes, were infinitely fuperior
"to thofe of Claude. John and Andrew always lived
"in the greateft unity; and their pictures, though done
"by two different hands, feemed but the work of one.
"John Both had the misfortune, in 1650, to lofe his
"brother, who drowned himfelf; and John died of
"grief, the fame year, at the age of forty.

"*Peter de Laar*, was furnamed the Bamboche, in Ita-
"ly, becaufe of his uncouth form, or rather becaufe he
"was the author of that fpecies of grotefque painting,
"in which we find thofe kind of figures, called Bambo-
"chades. He travelled into France and Italy, and died
"at Harlem 167 ç, aged fixty-two (*a*).

"John

(*a*) The celebrated Erafmus, born at Amfterdam, and fo well
known in the literary world, was an excellent Painter. The merit of his paintings is attefted by the Artifts of his time. He
ornamented the monaftery of Emmaus, which is now deftroyed
with his works; nor do we find that one of his pictures has
been preferved.

Adrian Vander Weff is the Painter, who, among the Dutch,
has difcovered moft tafte and genius. He was born at Rotterdam
in 1659 and applied himfelf to paint hiftory in fmall. The
Elector Palatine heaped benefits upon him, and created him a
Knight. Vander Weff died at Amfterdam in the year 1727.
There is a great collection of Paintings by this Artift at Duffeldorp. Among them there is one which is a mafter-piece of expreffion: it reprefents Chrift on the Crofs, the Virgin fainting,

" *John Cousin* may be looked upon as the first French
" Painter of eminence. He was born near Sens, lived in
" 1589,

and Magdalen kneeling, weeping, and looking at the Virgin.
The figure of Magdalen is admirable for it's pathos and reality.

There are several Painters at present in Flanders, of superior
merit. Among others are, M. Lyens at Brussels ; M. Heryens,
at Malines ; and M. Varagen, at Louvain ; all three History
Painters. The latter is indebted to himself only for his talents,
and to the generosity of M. Lyens for his celebrity. All the
Painters of Flanders were astonished, to see excellent pictures in
circulation, the author of which was unknown. The freshness of
the colouring informed them they were newly painted, yet all in-
quiries to know where they came from were fruitless. M. Lyens,
more struck than the rest by this singularity, determined, if possible, to discover this anonymous Painter, who deserved so well to
be known ; and for this purpose travelled through the towns of
Flanders, and asked all the young Painters he could get any intelligence of. He came at last o Louvain, which town he was
ready to quit, without finding what he was in search of. He happened however to be told, there was another man in Louvain
who busied himself about Painting, but who worked merely for
subsistence ; was unknown to every body, and, no doubt, a poor
Dauber, as execrable as obscure. M. Lyens determined to visit
the man, whose wife every day kept a stall in the street, where she
sold matches. The husband was shut up in his garret, whither
M. Lyens mounted. The lodging, and simplicity of the man,
gave no new animation to his hopes : he asked, however, to see a
picture.----I have but one, said the man ; there is a deal of work
in it, and it is very dear.----What is the price ?---Oh, I must have
four guineas for it ; I cannot afford it for less ; I have been at
work on it these three months.----Well, let me see it.----The good

man

" 1589, and acquired great reputation during the reigns
" of Henry II. Francis II. Charles IX. and Henry III.
" He practised Sculpture with fuccefs, underftood Ma-
" thematics and Anatomy, and was an able Architect.
" He painted much on glafs, which was then in great
" efteem; and likewife on canvas.

" *Simon Vouet* died 1641. Moft of the eminent French
" Painters of the laft age were his fcholars. Such were
" Le Bruur, Le Sueur, Le Valentin, Jean-Baptifte Mole,
" Aubin, Claude Vouet, François Perrier, Pierre Mig-
" nard, Nicolas Chaperon, Charles Poerfon, Dorigny,
" the father, Louis and Henri Teftelin, Alphonfe Du-
" frefnoi, and many others.

" *Charles Alphonfe Dufrefnoi*, was a good Poet, a good
" Painter, an able Architect, and underftood Latin,
" Greek, and the Mathematics. No Painter came fo
" near Titian as Dufrefnoi. He has left a beautiful

man brought out his picture, and prefented it to M. Lyens, who
inftantly exclaimed, with tranfport, *I have found him at laft!*

The reft of the converfation added to the aftonifhment of M.
Lyens, who learnt, this excellent Painter had never had a mafter: that he was the Scholar of Nature only: that he had never
fufpected his own fuperiority; and that he had conftantly fold his
pictures, for fifteen years, to a fellow, who had been difhoneft
enough to take advantage of his fituation and fimplicity; and
give him a vile price for pictures, which he fold excefsively dear.
M. Lyens had the glory to draw talents from obfcurity, which he
knew how to admire. He introduced M. Vargen to the world,
who owes the reputation and wealth he at prefent poffeffes, to this
generous Artift.

L 4

" poem

" poem on Painting, which has been translated into all
" languages. He died in 1665.

" *Claude Gelée*, called Lorrain, was a famous Land-
" fcape Painter, born in the diocefe of Toul in Lorrain,
" and died at Rome in 1682, aged eighty-two.

" *Sebeſtian Bourdon*, a great French Painter, died at
" Paris in 1671, aged fifty-five. There are many of his
" works in Paris: among others, the crucifixion of St.
" Peter in the church of Notre-Dame, which is thought
" to be his chef-d'œuvre.

" *Euſtache le Sueur*, born at Paris in 1617, became a
" fublime Painter, without ever having feen Italy. The
" paintings of the Cloiſter of the Chartreux at Paris, by
" him, have occaſioned him to be compared to Raphael.

" The celebrated *le Brun* was born at Paris, and died
" in 1690. At twelve years old he painted his grand-
" father's portrait. In the collection of the Palais-
" Royal, are two pictures painted by him at fourteen;
" one is Hercules taming the horfes of Diomede; the
" other that fame hero offering facrifice. Louis XIV.
" commanded him to paint the principal actions of his
" reign; and le Brun ingeniouſly and allegorically united
" Fable and Hiſtory, by which happy aſſemblage he
" formed a kind of epic poem of the acts of Louis, with
" which he enriched the Gallery at Verſailles. The
" King ordered le Brun likewife to ornament the Gal-
" lery of the Louvre, with the acts of Alexander the
" Great. Among the beſt paintings of this Artiſt are
" diſtinguiſhed the Martyrdom of St. Stephen and of
" St. Andrew at Notre-Dame; a Penitent Magdalen at
" the Carmelites, Rue Saint-Jacques; the Refurrection
" of Jefus Chriſt in the Church of St. Sepulchre, Rue
                                        " Saint-

" Saint-Denis; a Prefentation to the Temple of the
" Capuchins of the Fauxbourg, Saint-Jacques; the
" cieling of the Seminary Chapel of Saint-Sulpice,
" reprefenting the Affumption, and thought to be
" one of the beft of his works; the famous picture of
" Mofes prefenting the Brazen Serpent to the Ifraelites,
" in the Convent of Picpus; St. Charles kneeling, and
" imploring divine mercy for the city of Milan, at St.
" Nicolas du-Chardonneret ; the Maffacre of the In-
" nocents, at the Palais-Royal, &c.

" *Jean Jouvenet*, a great Painter, having received a
" paralytic ftroke in his right hand, came, by force of
" induftry, to paint equally well with his left. Reftout,
" the Nephew, was his beft fcholar. He died in 1717.

" *Antoine Coypel* was received a Member of the Academy
" of Painting at the age of twenty, and died in 1722.

" *Francois le Moine* was born at Paris. When he had
" painted the cupola of the Virgin's Chapel at the church
" of Saint-Sulpice, where he reprefented the Affumption,
" Louis XIV. chofe him to paint the Grand Saloon at
" Verfailles, which has fince been called the Saloon of
" Hercules. Le Moine there reprefented the apotheofis
" of this hero. This grand and magnificent compofition
" included more than one hundred and forty figures,
" fuftained on one bafe, in the midft of which are re-
" prefented the principal labours of Hercules, in coun-
" terfeit ftucco ; the whole work is diftributed into fe-
" veral groups, and was finifhed in 1736, after four years
" affiduous labour. It ought to be looked upon as the
" greateft in Europe, and as an immortal monument of
" the genius of its author. Violent grief deprived this
" great Artift of his reafon, and he died of feveral ftabs

L 5   " which

" which he gave himfelf with a fword in 1737, aged
" forty-nine. Le Moine made a fhort trip to Italy, but
" he only paffed fix months there. His principal fcholars
" were Boucher, Natoire, Nonotte, le Bel, and Challes.

" *Jean Petitot* is looked upon as the firft who brought
" Painting in enamel to perfection. He was born at Ge-
" neva, in 1607, and was originally a Jeweller. Vandyke
" having feen his works, advifed him to apply himfelf to
" Portrait Painting, and received him among his pupils.
" He foon obtained great perfection, and was affifted by
" Bordier, his brother in law, who painted the drapery,
" head-dreffes, &c. of his Portraits. Petitot was held in
" great eftimation by Charles I. of England. After the
" death of that Monarch, he attached himfelf to
" Charles II. and followed him to France. Louis XIV.
" retained this Painter in his fervice, and Petitot was
" received an Academician. He lived 36 years at Paris,
" where he divided a million (41,666l. fterling) with
" Bordier, which they had amaffed together, without
" ever having had the leaft difference. At the revoca-
" tion of the Edict of Nantes, Petitot retired into his
" own country, and died in 1691, at the age of 84, in the
" Canton of Berne."

For reafons before cited, I have thought it would not
be improper to add a lift of the principal Sculptors, ancient and modern, and a fmall abridgment of the Hiftory
of Architecture. I have taken thofe extracts from the
Encyclopædia, and have, as before, occafionally added
Notes from the Diary of my Travels, the exactitude of
which may be depended upon.

ANCIENT.

" The names of the Egyptian Sculptors have not come
" down to us; and the Greeks have effaced all thofe of
" Rome.

" *Appollonius* and *Taurifcus*, two Rhodians, conjointly
" executed the celebrated Antique of Zethus and Am-
" phion tying Dirce (*a*) to a Bull. It is all one block of
" marble, even to the very cords, is ftill in exiftence,
" and known by the name of the Farnefe Bull (*b*).

" *Phidias*, a native of Athens, flourifhed about the year
" of the world 3556, in the 83d Olympiad. It was he,
" who, after the Battle of Marathon, worked on a block
" of marble, which the Perfians, in expectation of vic-
" tory, had brought to erect as a trophy. He turned it
" into a *Nemefis*, the Goddefs whofe function it is to hum-
" ble haughty men. The chef-d'œuvre of Phidias was
" his Olympian Jove, which was thought one of the
" feven wonders of the world. Phidias was actuated and

(*a*) Dirce was Queen of Thebes, to marry whom Lycus had
repudiated Antiope. Jupiter fell in love with the latter, took the
form of Lycus to deceive her, and pretended a reconciliation.
Dirce believing Lycus vifited Antiope, imprifoned her, and made
her fuffer great hardfhips. Antiope, at laft, efcaped, and was
brought to bed of Zethus and Amphion, on Mount Cythero,
whom fhe delivered to the care of fhepherds. The young Princes,
at length, to revenge their mother, had the barbarity to tie Dirce
to the tail of a mad bull, and fhe was dafhed to pieces.----*Dict.
de la Fable.*

(*b*) It is much more remarkable for the prodigious fize of the
block of marble, than for the beauty of the workmanfhip.

L 6   " infpired

" inspired in the construction of this statue, by a spirit
" of vengeance against the Athenians, of whom he had
" a right to complain; and by a desire that his ungrate-
" ful country should not possess his best work, for he was
" then labouring for the Eleans. To honour the me-
" mory of the Artist, they created a new office in favour
" of his descendants, which was to take care of this
" statue. The statue was of gold and ivory, sixty feet
" high, and made every succeeding Sculptor despair of
" arriving at such excellence.

" The Athenian Minerva of Phidias, says Pliny, was
" twenty-six cubits high, of ivory and gold; on the
" borders of the Goddess's shield Phidias represented, in
" bass-relief the Combat of the Amazons; and within,
" that of the Gods and Giants. He depicted the Battle of
" the Centaurs, and Lapithæ on her buskins; and deco-
" rated the base of the statue by a basso-relievo of the birth
" of Pandora. The composition contained the birth of
" twenty other Gods; the Serpent and the Sphynx, on
" which the Goddess rested her lance, were particularly
" admired. These circumstances have only been de-
" scribed by Pliny, and indeed they were lost to the
" spectators; for the shield of Minerva being ten feet in
" diameter, these ornaments could not be seen distinctly
" enough to judge of their merit on a figure near forty
" feet high, and which was still raised higher by being
" placed on a pedestal; it was not therefore, in these
" small objects, that the principal merit of the statue
" of Minerva consisted.

" *Polycletes* was born at Sicyone, a city of Pelopon-
" nesus, and lived in the 87th Olympiad; his works
" were invaluable. That which acquired him the highest
" reputation,

" reputation, was the ftatue of Adoryphorus, that is to
" fay, a Guard of the King of Perfia. In this ftatue all
" the proportions of the human body were fo happily
" preferved, that they came from all parts to confult it
" as a perfect model; fo that it was called, by Judges,
" *The Rule.*

" *Zenodorus* flourifhed in the time of Nero, and was
" famed for a prodigious ftatue of Mercury, and after-
" wards for the Coloffus of Nero (*a*), which was 110 or
" 120 feet high; Vefpafian took away the head of Nero,
" and in its ftead placed the head of Apollo, adorned
" with feven rays, each of which were feven feet and a
" half long.

" The Venus de Medicis (*b*) bears the name of Cleo-
" menes, the fon of Apollodorus, the Athenian.

" The Farnefe Hercules ; bears that of Glycon, an
Athenian.

" The Pallas, in the Ludovifi gardens, at Rome; that
" of Antiochus, the fon of Illas.

" The Borghefe Gladiator; that of Agafias, the fon
" of Ofytheus, an Ephefian.

" The Torfus Belvidera (*c*), by Apollonius, the fon
" of Neftor, an Athenian.

" The

(*a*) One of the fineft ruins at Rome, the Colifeum, is faid to
have taken its name from this ftatue, which anciently ftood
there. The Gladiators fought in the Colifeum. Benedict XIV.
fpoilt the infide of this admirable monument of antiquity, by
building little chapels in it.

(*b*) This fine ftatue is at Florence, in the Gallery of the Grand
Duke.

(*c*) At Rome there is the trunk of a human figure, which is
called the Antique, or Herculean Torfus ; it is very famous, and
is

" The name of Callimachus is seen on a baſſo-relievo,
" repreſenting Bacchants and a Faun in the Albani
" Palace (a).

" The Apotheoſis of Homer, in the Colonna Palace,
" bears, on a vaſe, the name of Archelaus, the ſon of
" Apollonius.

" It is ſingular, as M. de Caylùs remarks, that, of all
" theſe names, only the four firſt are mentioned by
" Pliny; and ſtill more ſo, that none of theſe ſeven,
" ſtatues are noticed by him. The Laocoon (b) and the
" Dirce are the only remaining works of which he
" ſpeaks. On the other hand, we ought not to be ſur-
                                                    " prized

is in the Muſeum. The fighting Gladiator is in the Borgheſe
Palace, and the dying Gladiator in the Capitol.

(a) The Albani Palace is without the walls of Rome, and one
of the fineſt in Italy. It is immenſe, of moſt ſuperb architecture, and decorated with obeliſks, fountains, columns of precious
marble, baſſo-relievo, and moſt beautiful antique ſtatues. It contains ſome paintings, a cieling by Mengs, and one thing ſaid to
be Unique, which is an antique ſtatue of a female Satyr: ſuch a
figure being, as it is aſſerted, no where elſe to be found but in
Baſſo-relievo.

(b) Laocoon, the ſon of Priam and Hecuba, and High Prieſt of
Apollo, oppoſed the entrance of the Trojan horſe, but was over-
ruled. At the ſame time, two enormous ſerpents came from the
ſea, and aſſaulted his children at the foot of the Altar. He ran
to ſuccour them, and was ſtrangled with them, by the monſters
twiſting round their bodies.----Dict. de la Fable.

The Grecian Sculptor has taken the point of time, when, unable to get free from the Serpents, Laocoon and his children are
almoſt expiring. The ſculpture is thought admirable, though the
                                                    children

" prized at the filence of Paufanias, relative to all the
" beautiful ftatues of Rome ; when he travelled through
" Greece, they were tranfported into Italy, for the Ro-
" mans had been 300 years endeavouring to rob Greece
" of its Pictures and Statues.   The Roman Sculpture
" had but a fhort reign, and was never brought to fuch
" perfection.   It began to languifh under Tiberius, and
" the buft of Caracalla is looked upon as its expiring
" figh. It did not revive till the pontificate of Julius II.
" and Leo X. after which it was called *Modern Sculpture.*"

MODERN SCULPTORS.

" *Donato*, born at Florence, lived in the fifteenth cen-
" tury.   The Senate of Venice chofe him to make the
" Equeftrian ftatue in bronze, which the public erected to
" Gatamelata, the Grand Captain, who, from the loweft
" extraction, arrived to the rank of General of the Ve-
" netian armies, and gained feveral remarkable victories;
" but the Chef-d'œuvre of Donato was a Judith cutting
" off the head of Holofernes.

" *Roffi Propertia* flourifhed at Bologna, under the pon-
" tificate of Clement VII. Mufic was her amufement,
" Sculpture her occupation.   At firft fhe modelled her
" figures in clay, afterwards carved in wood, and at laft
" in ftone. She decorated the front of the church of St.
" Petrona with feveral ftatues in marble, which procured
" her great praife ; but an unhappy paffion for a young

children are faid to be too fmall. The moft beautiful and perfect
of all the Antique Statues is the Apollo Belvidera, which people,
ignorant of the art, cannot behold without admiration. Apollo
is reprefented juft after he has killed the Serpent Pithon.

" man,

" man, who was infenfible to her love, threw her into a
" kind of languor, that put an end to her days. Her
" beft and laft work was a baffo-relievo of Jofeph and Po-
" tiphar's wife.

" *Goujon*, a Parifian, flourifhed under the reigns of
" Francis I. and Henry II. A modern author has called
" him the *Corregio of Sculpture*, becaufe he always con-
" fulted the graces. No perfon better underftood figures
" of demi-relief, nor can any thing be finer in this way
" than his *Fontaine des Innocens*, Rue St. Denis, at
" Paris; the works of Goujon were feen at the gate of
" Saint Antoine; he was alfo a good Architect.

" *Nicolas Bachelier* was the Scholar of Michael An-.
" gelo; he lived at Touloufe, under the reign of
" Francis I. where he eftablifhed good tafte, and banifhed
" the Gothic manner, till then in ufe.

" *Baccio Bandinelli*, born at Florence, was greatly
" efteemed as a Sculptor. It was he who replaced the
" right-arm of the Laocoon; he died 1559.

" *John* of *Bologna* died at Florence, towards the be-
" ginning of the feventeenth century, and was an ex-
" cellent Painter; he ornamented the public fquare of
" Florence with that marble groupe which is ftill there
" to be feen, of the Rape of the Sabines. The Horfe,
" on which the ftatue of Henry IV. has fince been placed,
" in the middle of the Pont-Neuf, at Paris, is by him.

" *John Gonelli*, furnamed the Blind, of Cambaffi,
" from the place of his birth, in Tufcany, died at Rome,
" under the pontificate of Urban VIII. He was the
" Scholar of Pietro Tacca, and difcovered genius, but
" loft his fight at the age of 20. This misfortune did
" not prevent him from exercifing his art, which he did
" by

" by feeling alone. The statue of Cosmo I. Grand Duke
" of Tuscany, was thus performed by him, and he had
" equal success in various other of his works.

Pierre Puget, an admirable Sculptor, good Painter,
" and an excellent Architect, was born at Marseilles in
" 1623; he embellished Toulon, Marseilles, and Aix,
" with various Pictures, which still do honour to the
" churches of the Capuchins and the Jesuits; such are
" his Annunciation, his Baptism of Constantine, and
" his Picture called the Saviour of the world. The
" Education of Achilles was his last Painting. The Cro-
" tonian Milo is the first and best statue which was seen
" at Versailles, done by Puget. This admirable Artist
" died at Marseilles in 1694, aged 72.

" *Jacques Sarazin*, born at Noyon, was contemporary
" with Puget. The tomb of Cardinal Berulli, in the
" church of the Carmelites, Fauxbourg Saint-Jacques,
" is by this excellent Artist. Among his works at Ver-
" sailles we ought not to forget Remus and Romulus
" suckled by a goat, and another group at Marli, in
" equal estimation, representing Two Children at Play
" with a He-Goat.

" *Theodon*, born in France in the seventeenth century,
" was an able Sculptor.

" *Algardi*, an Italian, flourished about the middle of
" the 17th century. Among other works of this superior
" Artist, his Basso-relievo is much admired, which re-
" presents St. Peter and St. Paul in the clouds, menacing
" Attilla, going to sack Rome. This Basso-relievo serves
" as a Picture to one of the small altars of the great
" church of St. Peter.

" *Michael*

" *Michael Anguier*, died in 1680, and was the brother
" of Francis Anguier, who, like himfelf, was alfo a dif-
" tinguifhed Artift ; he is well known for his marble
" Amphitheatre in the park at Verfailles ; his works at
" the gate of Saint Denis ; his figures at the portal of
" the Val-de-Grace ; and by various others.

" *John-Lawrence Bernini*, called the Cavalier Bernini,
" was born at Naples, in 1598. Louis XIV. invited him
" to Paris in 1665.

" *François Desjardins*, a native of Breda, died in 1694.
" He executed the monument of *La Place de Victoires*, at
" Paris.

" *François Girardon*, born at Troye, in Champagne,
" has almoft equalled antiquity by his Baths of Apollo ;
" his tomb of Cardinal de Richelieu, which is in the
" church of the Sorbonne ; and by his Statue of
" Louis XIV. which ftands in the Place Vendôme ; he
" made alfo a good Buft of Boileau. Girardon died in
" 1698.

" *Jean-Baptifte Tuby*, called the Roman, holds a dif-
" tinguifhed rank among the Artifts who appeared un-
" der the reign of Louis XIV. The Maufoleum of the
" Vifcount de Turenne, interred at Saint Denis, was
" defigned by le Brun, and executed by Tuby. Immor-
" tality is feen holding a crown with one hand, and
" fuftaining Turenne with the other ; Wifdom and Vir-
" tue ftand on each fide him ; the firft aftonifhed at the
" fatal ftroke, which robbed France of this hero ; the
" other plunged in confternation. Tuby died at Paris
" in 1700.

" *Zumbo*,

" *Zumbo*, born at Syracufe, had no other mafter but
" his own genius; he worked wholly in coloured wax,
" which he prepared after a particular manner. Warren
" and le Bel knew the fecret before him, but the works
" of our Artift excelled all others of this kind. Zumbo
" executed, for the Grand Duke of Tufcany, that re-
" nowned fubject la Corruzione (the Corruption;) a
" work curious for its exactitude and great natural
" knowledge. It confifts of five figures, coloured after
" nature: the firft reprefents a dying man, the fecond a
" corpfe, the third the body beginning to putrify, the
" fourth putrefaction advanced, and the fifth putre-
" trefaction at its height, which cannot be beheld with-
" out a kind of horror. The Grand Duke placed the
" work in his Cabinet (*a*). Zumbo died at Paris, in
" 1701.

" *John-Balthazar Keller*, incomparable in the art of
" cafting in bronze, was born at Zurich. He came to
" France, where, on the laft day of December, 1692,
" he produced his Equeftrian Statue of Louis XIV. (*b*)
" which is twenty feet high, and all one piece, as may be
" feen in the Place Vendôme. There are other admira-
" ble works of his in the gardens of Verfailles, and elfe-
" where. Louis XIV. made him Intendant of the Ar-
" fenal Foundery. He died in 1702. His brother, Jean-
" Jaques, was alfo very fkilful in the fame profeffion.

" *Pierre le Gros* was born at Paris, in 1666, and died at
" Rome in 1719; in which city he had a part in the moft

(*a*) At Florence, where it is ftill to be feen.

(*b*) *There is fome inaccuracy in the account of this ftatue; it has
juft before been attributed to* François Girardon. T.

" fuperb

" fuperb pieces of Sculpture that capital of the fine arts
" has produced.　Such are his Louis Gonzago, over the
" altar of the Roman College, which has been engraved ;
" his Baffo-relievo of Mount-Piety ; his Tomb of Cardinal
" Caffanata; his Statue of Staniflaus Kofka, in the No-
" viciate of the Jefuits (a); and his Triumph of Religion
" over Herefy, in the church of Giezu.　The Bafs-re-
" lievo, in the church of *Saint Jaque des Incurables*, at
" Paris, by this Artift, is well known.

" *Antoine Coyfevox* was born at Lyons, in 1640.　The
" great ftair-cafe, the garden, and the gallery, at Ver-
" failles, are ornamented by his Sculpture.　Several of
" the Tombs which decorate the churches at Paris are
" by him ; his two prodigious groups, of Mercury and
" Fame, fitting on winged horfes, are well known ; they
" were placed in the gardens at Marli, in 1702; each

" group, fuftained by a trophy, was cut from a block of
" marble ; and this celebrated Artift laboured with fuch
" furprizing fire, and a correctnefs fo uncommon, that
" he compleated them both in two years.　However,
" perhaps, the work would fuffer, if compared with the
" Marcus Curtius of Bernini, at Verfailles.　Coyfevox
" died in 1720.

" *Nicholas Coufton* was born at Lyons, in 1658, and
" died in 1733 ; he was the Scholar of Coyfevox. With-

(*a*) Called at prefent St. Andrew's.　The Statue of Le Gros
has great reputation, and affords fine touches, but it wants expreffion　The face is too flefhy, the hands too fat, and the figure
is a Picture of Sleep rather than Pain.　The Saint is in his religious habit; his gown is black marble, the reft white.　We have
before obferved this is falfe tafte.

" ont

" out entering into a detail of his works, it will be suf-
" ficient to cite the fine Statue of the Emperor Commo-
" dus, under the form of Hercules, in the gardens at
" Verfailles. The Pedeſtrian Statue of Julius Cæſar, the
" Rivers Seine and Marne, in the Tuilleries, and the
" Vow of Louis XIII. behind the high altar of Notre
" Dame, at Paris. His name, celebrated in the arts, is
" likewiſe ſuſtained with great diſtinction, by Meſſieurs
" Couſtou, who belonged to the ſame Academy.——
" There have been many other good Sculptors."

ARCHITECTURE.

" Ancient authors allow the Egyptians to have firſt
" built with ſymmetry and proportion, but Greece
" ought to be regarded as the birth-place of
" good Architecture (a). Among the Romans, it
" arrived at its higheſt perfection in the time of Au-
" guſtus (b); it began to be neglected under Tiberius
" and Nero; was raiſed again by Trajan, and protected
" by Alexander Severus, who could not impede its
" downfall with the Empire of the Weſt; from the ruins
" of which it did not riſe again for ſeveral ages. It then
" took a new form called Gothic, which ſubſiſted wholly
" till Charlemagne endeavoured to re-eſtabliſh the an-
" cient mode. Architecture afterwards became as much
" too light as it before had been too heavy; the Builders
" of thoſe times placed their beauties in a delicacy and

(a) The beſt days of Architecture among the Greeks, was the
Age of Pericles.

(b) The famous Pantheon was built under the reign of Auguſtus.

" profuſion

" profusion of ornaments till then unknown; which
" taste they received from the Arabs and Moors, who
" brought it into France from the Southern Countries, as
" the Goths and Vandals had brought the heavy Gothic
" from the North.   It is only within these two last cen-
" turies, that the Architects of France and Italy have
" applied themselves to recover the beauty, simplicity,
and proportion of ancient Architecture."

The continuation of this Extract is taken from an
estimable work, in two volumes, entitled *Vies des Archi-
tectes Anciens & Modernes*; translated from the Italian,
by M. Pingeron.

Besides the six orders of Architecture, says M. Pingeron, there are two other bastard ones, called the Attic
and the Cariatic; the last of which thus took its rise.

" The Carians having joined the Persians, the other
" Greeks declared against them, took their city, put
" their men to the sword, and carried away their women
" captive.   Not contented to lead them like slaves, in
" the triumphs of their Generals, they insisted that their
" Architects should sustain the entablatures of their
" public buildings, by figures of women, representing
" the Carians; and these were substituted instead of
" columns. The Lacedæmonians did the same thing after
" the battle of Platea: they built a vast gallery, which
" they called *Persian*, the roof of which was sustained by
" Statues, habited like the Captives they had taken
" from the Persians.

" History informs us, Ninus built Nineveh, the form
" of which city was a parallelogram, or oblong square,
" twenty-four French leagues in circumference; and it's
" walls were so thick, three chariots might drive abreast
" upon them.   They were 100 feet high, and were de-
                                    " fended

" fended by 1500 towers, each 100 feet high. Semira-
" mis, not contented with this vaſt city, built in its
" neighbourhood the famous Babylon, perfectly ſquare,
" each ſide of which was five French leagues, and en-
" cloſed it within twenty-five gates of braſs. The Eu-
" phrates ran through the midſt of it; and at it's two
" extremities ſtood the ſovereign Palaces, which were
" ſurrounded by Terraces ſuſtained by Arcades. The
" magnificent Temple of Jupiter Belus was at Babylon,
" which was 212 fathoms high, and the ſame breadth at
" the baſe. It conſiſted of eight ſquare towers, placed
" one upon the other, and diminiſhed by degrees. The
" ſpectator might ſuppoſe he there beheld the remains of
" the famous Tower of Babel, which St. Jerome thinks
" was built to the height of three miles, 3379 fathoms.
" Some pretend, that Ninus, Belus, and Semiramis not
" only commanded theſe enormous works, but made
" plans of them, and preſided at their execution.

" *Trophonius* and *Agameda*, who lived 1400 years be-
" fore Chriſt, were the firſt Grecian Architects men-
" tioned in Hiſtory.

" *Theodorus*, who lived ſeven hundred years before
" Chriſt, was an Architect and Sculptor, and is ſaid to
" be the inventor of locks, the rule, the level, and the
" turning lath (a).

" *Satyrus* and *Petus* deſigned and built the tomb
" which Artemiſa erected in Halicarnaſſus, to Mauſoleus,
" King of Caria.

" *Dinocrates* was the Architect that Alexander em-
" ployed in the building of Alexandria.

(a) Calus, the nephew of Dedalus, whom Ovid calls Perdix,
invented the ſaw and the compaſs.

" *Coſſutius*

" *Coffutius* was the firſt Roman Architect who built
" after the manner of the Greeks, 200 years before
" Chriſt.

" *Vitruvius* lived under the reign of Auguſtus, to
" whom he dedicated his Treatiſe on Architecture. This
" Treatiſe is come down to us.

" *Apollodorus* conſtructed the famous Trajan Pillar;
" but the moſt celebrated work of Trajan and Apollo-
" dorus was, the bridge they built over the Danube, in
" the Lower Hungary, veſtiges of which ſtill remain. It
" was more than 300 feet high, and about 800 perches
" long, which make half a league. The two extremi-
" ties of the bridge were defended by two fortreſſes, yet
" this bridge is nothing when compared to thoſe which
" might be ſeen in China. Among others, we are told
" of one with a hundred arches, ſo high, that a veſſel
" may paſs under in full ſail. It is built of large blocks
" of white marble, over which is a balluſtrade, with pe-
" deſtals on each ſide of marble lions. There are many
" bridges in China, to paſs from one mountain to ano-
" ther. Near Kin-tung is a wooden-bridge, ſupported
" by twenty chains, faſtened at each end to a moun-
" tain.

" After the death of Trajan, Adrian built a Temple
" from his own deſigns. He ſent his plans to Apollo-
" dorus, who replied, that if the Goddeſſes and other
" Statues, which were ſeated in the Temple, ſhould take
" a fancy to riſe, they would run the riſk of breaking
" their heads againſt the cieling. This criticiſm is ſaid
" to have coſt him his life.

" *Nicon*, father to the famous Phyſician Galen, was
" alſo an Architect. Galen himſelf had ſome know-

" ledge

" ledge of Architecture, and wrote well on it's prin-
" ciples.

" *Sennamar*, an Arabian Architect, lived in the fif-
" teenth century. He built two Palaces, one of which
" was called Sadir, and the other Khaovarnack, which
" the Arabs place among the wonders of the world ; and
" with juſtice, if what they ſay be not fabulous. One
" ſingle ſtone ſuſtained, they knew not how, every part
" of the edifice ; ſo that had that ſtone been taken away,
" the building muſt have fallen in ruins.

" *Antenius*, in conjunction with Iſidorus of Milet,
" built the famous Temple of Sancta Sophia, at Conſtan-
" tinople, by order of the Emperor Juſtinian. This vaſt
" edifice was firſt built by Conſtantine, but was burnt
" and rebuilt ſeveral times. Juſtinian determined to
" make it a magnificent Temple : it's ſcite is on the
" ſummit of a little hill, that overlooks the city ; the
" plan is almoſt a perfect ſquare, for it is 252 feet
" long, and 228 wide ; from the centre of the cupola to
" to the floor is 80 feet ; it is full of Pillars of Marble,
" Porphyry, &c. and has nine magnificent gates of
" Bronze. Alabaſter, Porphyry, Ophites, Mother-of-
" Pearl, and Cornelian are not ſpared within or with-
" out this edifice. Antenius was not only the Architect,
" but the Sculptor likewiſe ; and alſo a ſkilful Mechanic.

" *Buſquetto*, of Grecian origin, was entruſted with the
" building of the Cathedral at Piſa in 1016, which is
" one of the moſt beautiful of that age.

" *Williams*, a German, in 1174, built, with Bonano
" and Thomonazo, two Piſan Sculptors, the famou
" Steeple of Piſa. This edifice, which is entirely of
" marble, is 250 palms high. It owes it's fame to

" it's inclination, which is seventeen palms (a) out of a
" right line, and was the consequence of an accident
" during it's construction. The same accident happened
" to the Tower of Garisendi, at Bologna; the inclina-
" tion of the latter, however, is not so great.

" *Suger Abbot*, of Saint Dennis, was said to be one of
" the ablest architects of his time.

" *Robert de Covey*, who died 1311, finished the Church
" of Saint Nicaise, at Rheims, which is esteemed for the
" delicacy of it's ornaments, and the beauty of it's pro-
" portions.

" *William Wickham*, an Englishman, who died in 1404,
" gave the plan of Windsor-Castle, and of the magnifi-
" cent Cathedral at Winchester.

" *Brunelleschi*, a Florentine, who died in 1440, was a
" celebrated Architect, and built the palace Pitti, at
" Florence, in which the Grand Duke of Tuscany resides.

" *Bramanti* died in 1514. The round little Temple,
" so much admired in the midst of the cloister of Saint
" Peter Montorio, is one of the most esteemed works
" of Bramanti. Bramanti laid the foundation of Saint
" Peter's at Rome; but his successors made so many al-
" terations, that his plans have little to do with the
" building.

" *Sansovin*, who died in 1570, was a famous Architect.
" His best work is the library of Saint Mark's, at Venice.

" *Philibert de l'Orme* was born at Lyons, and died in
" 1577. He endeavoured to abolish the Gothic Archi-
" tecture, and substitute the Grecian. The horse-shoe
" stair-case at Fontainbleau, is by de l'Orme.

(a) The palm, where it is the usual measure, is about eight
inches three lines French.

" *Vignoli*

" *Vignoli* was born in Modena, and died in 1573. He
" wrote a Treatise on the Five Orders of Architecture.

" *Vasari*, an Italian, who died in 1574, was a good
" Painter and Architect.

" *Palladio*, a famous Architect, was born at Vicenza,
" and died in 1580. Venice is full of his works. The
" celebrated Olympic Theatre of Vicenza is by him.

" *Bartholomew Ammanati*, a Florentine, died in 1586,
" was eminent in Sculpture, and gained great reputa-
" tion in Architecture. It was he who finished the Pitti
" Palace.

" *Constantine Servi*, a Florentine, who died in 1622,
" was a Painter, Engineer, and Architect. The Great
" Sophy of Persia asked him of the Grand Duke Cosmo II.
" and he remained a year in Persia, but what he did there
" is not known.

" *Jacques Desbrosses*, a celebrated French Architect in
" the time of Mary de Medicis, gave the plan of the
" Luxembourg Palace. The design which this Artist also
" gave for the Façade of the Church of Saint Gervais,
" is highly spoken of: it contains three orders; the sta-
" tues are heavy, and ill executed. Desbrosses also con-
" structed the famous Aqueduct of Arcueil.

" *Inigo Jones* was born at London, and died in 1652.
" His principal works are the Banqueting-House, White-
" hall, Lindsey Palace, the Church of St. Paul's Co-
" vent Garden, &c. &c. The Architect Webb was his
" son-in-law and pupil.

" *François Monsard* was born at Paris, and died in
" 1666; he laid the foundation of Val de-Grace; and is
" said to be the inventor of those apartments next the
" roof, which the French call A la Mansard.

" *James Van-Campen*, a Dutchman, died in 1638. He

" rebuilt, in a moſt majeſtic ſtyle, the Town-houſe of
" Amſterdam, after it had been burnt down. This is the
" fineſt edifice in all Holland. He painted alſo; but, as
" he was rich and of a noble family, he took no pecuni-
" ary rewards for his Paintings and Deſigns.

" *François Boromini*, an Italian, died in 1667. He
" embelliſhed the Spada Palace, and built a colonade
" gallery, the perſpective of which makes it appear three
" times longer than it really is. The decorations of this
" gallery gave the Cavalier Bernini the idea of the fa-
" mous *Scala Regia* (a).

The *Cavalier Bernini* died in 1680. He was the ſon of
" a Sculptor, and at ten years of age carved a marble
" head, ſtill to be ſeen at Saint Praxeda, which well me-
" rits the ſuffrages of all connoiſſeurs. Pope Paul V.
" would ſee him at work, and Bernini finiſhed in his
" preſence the model of a St. Paul's head, in half an
" hour. Bernini was ſcarce ſeventeen, when Rome, al-
" ready poſſeſſed ſeveral beautiful works of his compo-
" ſition. Among which is the Daphne and Apollo.
" When Urban VIII. became Pope, he ſaid to Bernini,
" *You are very happy to have ſeen the Cardinal Maffeo*
" *Barbarini elevated to the pontificate, but his happi-*
" *neſs is ſuperior to your's, ſince Bernini lives under his*
" *reign.* Bernini applied himſelf at once to Painting,
" Sculpture, and Architecture; he executed the Confeſ-
" ſion of Saint Peter in bronze (b); the Fountain of the
" Square of Navoni, and four Coloſſal Figures, repre-
" ſenting the Four Principal Rivers of the Earth, the
" Nile, the Danube, the Euphrates, and the Niger. Theſe

(a) The Connoiſſeurs hold Poromini to be an Architect of ill
taſte, and without genius.

(b) That is to ſay, the Canopy, Altar, &c. of Saint Peter.

" figures

" figures fit on an enormous mafs of rocks, whence the
" water falls.   The fame Artift gave the defign of the
" Fountain *Barcacia* (Bad Bark) which is at Rome in
" the Spanifh Square.   Bernini was famous for many
" other works.   The fuperb Stair-cafe befide Saint Pe-
" ter, the idea of which he took, as it is faid, from Bo-
" romini's fmall Gallery (*a*), and the charming Church
" of the Noviciate of the Jefuits, at Rome, are by Ber-
" nini.   One of his beft things in Sculpture, is Saint
" Therefa in an Ecftacy, with an Angel piercing her
" Heart with a flaming Dart.   It is at Rome, in the
" Church of Notre-Dame de la Victoire (*b*).   Bernini
" looked upon the famous Torfus as the moft perfect
" remain of antiquity.   Bernini was active, laborious,
" ardent, and paffionate ; but a good Chriftian, charitable
" and virtuous.   He loved the ftage, and played Comedy
" impromptu, in a fuperior manner ; he came into France,
" where he received many marks of diftinction from
" Louis XIV. (*c*).

" *Claude Perrault*, a French Architect, who died in

(*a*) He alfo built Saint Peter's Square and Colonade, and the
Tombs ef Urban VIII. and Alexander VII. in Saint Peter's
Church, are by him.   The latter is over a door in a dark place,
like a fpecies of cave ; Bernini has taken advantage of this po-
fition, and let a curtain fall over the door, which Death, beneath, raifes, and half fhews himfelf ; the Pope enters, with
Truth and Charity on each fide.   The one fhews him the fright-
ful fpectre approaching, the other confoles and encourages him.

(*b*) The expreffion of Saint Therefa's face is fublime, the figure of
the Angel delightful, but the Saint's drapery is too full of fmall folds
and bad.   It is fituated in a niche, over which is a window, which
gives a brilliancy to the Angel that produces a very happy effect.

(*c*) The Buft of Louis XIV. and the Statue of Marcus Curtius, beyond the room of the Swifs, at Verfailles, are by Bertini.

" 1683,

" 1688, was at once a Physician, Anatomist, Experi
" mental Philosopher, Painter, Musician, Engineer, and
" Architect. This learned man drew a design for the
" Façade of the Louvre, which deserved the preference
" over all the others that were presented. This superb
" Façade surprized Bernini, and is in fact the finest piece
" of Architecture to be seen in any sovereign palace of
" Europe. Perrault invented some very ingenious ma-
" chines, to carry and raise enormous stones; he also
" constructed a superb triumphal arch, which stood at
" the gate of Saint Antoine; likewise the Observatory,
" which is the finest in Europe. When Perrault was
" admitted a member of the *Academie des Sciences*, he no
" longer practised physic, except for his family, his
" friends, and the poor. He published four volumes,
" entitled *Essais de Physique*; likewise a collection of the
" machines he had invented. Charles Perrault, the
" brother of the Architect, wrote the famous Parallel
" between the Ancients and the Moderns, where he gave
" the preference entirely to the latter; which drew
" down the hatred of Boileau on both the brothers.
" Perrault endeavoured, with a crowd of French Ar-
" tists, to seek for a new order of Architecture; but
" discovered nothing, except a Corinthian Capital, the
" foliage of which was ridiculously replaced by ostrich
" plumes of feathers, while the columns represented
" trunks of trees.

" *François Blondel* died in 1688. The Gates of Saint
" Dennis, and Saint Antoine, at Paris, are by him; the
" first very beautiful (*a*); the second, only remarkable
" for some of the Sculpture.

(*a*) Blondel wrote all the Latin inscriptions on this gate; he
was likewise a great Mathematician.

" *Jules-*

" *Jules-Hardouin Manfard,* fon to the fifter of Fran-
" çois Manfard, took the name of that Architect ;
" his great work is the chateau of Verfailes. The plan
" of the Place des Victoires was his, and he finished the
" famous church *des Invalides* (began by *Liberal Bru-*
" *ant*) and built the Cupola, which is the fineft in Paris.
" He died in 1708.

" *François* Galli *Bibiena,* an Italian, died in 1739,
" and, as well as his brother, was a celebrated Painter
" and Architect He built the beautiful Theatre at
" Verona.

" *Chriftopher Wren,* an Englifhman (*a*), died in 1723.
" This Artift, at the age of fixteen, had made difcove-
" ries in Aftronomy and Mechanics. He was the Ar-
" chitect of the famous St. Paul's, London; which was
" begun in 1672, and finished in 1710; he laid the firft
" ftone himfelf, and his fon the laft.

" *Jacques Gabriel,* born at Paris, died in 1742, and
" began the Pont Royal (*b*), which was finished by Le
" Frére Romain.

" *Nicholas Salvi,* an Italian, was a Poet and Archi-
" tect, and died in 1751.

" *Boffrand,* who conftructed the famous Well of the
" Bicêtre, died in 1754 (*c*).

This catalogue might be much extended, for the author from whom it is extracted, cites many great Ita-

(*a*) *Sir Chriftopher—He received the honour of Knight-.*
hood. T.

(*b*) *A bridge at Paris.* T.

(*c*) It's depth is 171 feet, it's diameter 15, and 9 of inexhauft-
ible water ; for the bottom is a rock, which is the fource. A
retreat has been dug in the fide, two fathoms above the level of
the water, fix feet high, fupported all round by iron, to contain
workmen, tools, and every thing neceffary for repairs.

" lian

lian Lords, who have applied themselves wholly to the study of Architecture, in which they have excelled. He does not, however, mention a very celebrated modern, Vanvitelli, who made the elegant and magnificent Stair-case of the new Caserti Palace, near Naples, belonging to the King. Vanvitelli has been dead nine or ten years.

(3) He is called the Prince of Palagonia. His palace is near Palermo, and is thus described by Mr. Brydone, an English Traveller.

" —— " I shall therefore only speak of one, which, for
" it's singularity, certainly is not to be paralleled on
" the face of the earth: it belongs to the Prince of
" P——, a man of immense fortune, who has devoted
" his whole life to the study of monsters and chimeras,
" greater and more ridiculous than ever entered into the
" imagination of the wildest writers of romance or
" knight-errantry.

" The amazing crowd of statues that surround his
" house, appear, at a distance, like a little army drawn
" up for it's defence; but when you get amongst them,
" and every one assumes it's true likeness, you imagine
" you have got into the regions of delusion and enchant-
" ment; for, of all that immense group, there is not
" one made to represent any object in nature; nor is the
" absurdity of the wretched imagination that created
" them, less astonishing than it's wonderful fertility. It
" would require a volume to describe the whole, and a
" sad volume indeed it would make. He has put the
" heads of men to the bodies of every sort of animal, and
" the heads of every other animal to the bodies of men.
" Sometimes he makes a compound of five or six ani-
" mals, that have no sort of resemblance in nature. He
                                    " puts

" puts the head of a Lion to the neck of a Goose, the
" body of a Lizard, the legs of a Goat, the tail of a
" Fox. On the back of this monster, he puts another,
" if possible, still more hideous, with five or six heads,
" and a bush of horns ; they beat the beast in the Reve-
" lations all to nothing. There is no kind of horn in
" the world that he has not collected ; and his pleasure
" is, to see them all flourishing upon the same head.
" This is a strange species of madness ; and it is truly
" unaccountable, that he has not been shut up many
" years ago : but he is perfectly innocent, and troubles
" nobody by the indulgence of his phrenzy. On the
" contrary, he gives bread to a number of Statuaries,
" and other workmen, whom he rewards in proportion
" as they can bring their imaginations to coincide with
" his own ; or, in other words, according to the hide-
" ousness of the monsters they produce. It would be
" idle and tiresome to be particular in an account of
" these absurdities. The statues that adorn, or rather
" deform the great avenue, and surround the Court of
" the Palace, amount already to 600 ; notwithstanding
" which, it may be truly said, that he has not broken
" the second Commandment ; for of all that number,
" there is not the likeness of any thing in heaven above,
" in the earth beneath, or in the waters under the
" earth. The old ornaments, which were put up by his
" father, who was a sensible man, appear to have been
" in a good taste. They have all been knocked to pieces,
" and laid together in a heap, to make room for this new
" creation.

" The inside of this enchanted Castle corresponds ex-
" actly with the out ; it is in every respect as whimsical
" and fantastical ; and you cannot turn yourself to any
" side,

" fide, where you are not ftared in the face by fome hi-
" deous figure or other. Some of the apartments are
" fpacious and magnificent, with high arched roofs;
" which, inftead of plaifter or ftucco, are compofed en-
" tirely of large mirrors, nicely joined together. The
" effect that thefe produce (as each of them make a full
" angle with the other) is exactly that of a multiplying-
" glafs; fo that when three or four people are walk-
" ing below, there is always the appearance of three
" or four hundred walking above. The whole of the
" doors are likewife covered over with fmall pieces of
" mirror, cut into the moft ridiculous fhapes, and in-
" termixed with a great variety of cryftal and glafs of
" different colours. All the chimney-pieces, windows,
" and fide-boards, are crowded with pyramids, and
" pillars of tea-pots, caudle-cups, bowls, cups, faucers,
" &c. ftrongly cemented together: Some of thefe columns
" are not without their beauty; one of them has a large
" china chamber-pot for its bafe, and a circle of pretty
" little flower-pots for its capital; the fhaft of the co-
" lumn, upwards of four feet long, it compofed entirely
" of tea-pots of different fizes, diminifhed gradually
" from the bafe to the capital. The profufion of china
" that has been employed in forming thefe columns is
" incredible; I dare fay, there is not lefs than forty
" pillars and pyramids formed in this ftrange fantaftic
" manner.

" Moft of the rooms are paved with fine marble tables
" of different colours, that look like fo many tomb-
" ftones. Some of thefe are richly wrought with lapis
" lazuli, porphyry, and other valuable ftones: their
" fine polifh is now gone, and they only appear like
" common marble. The place of thefe beautiful tables
　　　　　　　　　　　　　　　　　　　　　　　" he

" he has supplied by a new set of his own invention,
" some of which are not without their merit.   These are
" made of the finest tortoise-shell, mixed with mother-of-
" pearl, ivory, and a variety of metals; and are mounted
" on fine stands of solid brass.

" The windows of this enchanted Castle are com-
" posed of a variety of glass of every different colour,
" mixed without any sort of order or regularity.   Blue,
" red, green, yellow, purple, violet.   So that at each
" window, you may have the heavens and earth of
" whatever colour you chuse, only by looking through
" the pane that pleases you.

" The house Clock is cased in the body of the Statue;
" the eyes of the figure move with the pendulum, turn-
" ing up their white and black alternately, and making
" a hideous appearance.

" His bed-chamber and dressingroom are like two apart-
" ments in Noah's Ark; there is scarce a beast, however
" vile, that he has not placed there; toads, frogs, ser-
" pents, lizards, scorpions, all cut out in marble, of their
" respective colours.   There are a great many busts too,
" that are not less singularly imagined.—Some of these
" make a very handsome profile on one side; turn to
" the other, and you have a skeleton.   Here you see a
" nurse with a child in her arms; its back is exactly
" that of an infant; its face is that of a wrinkled old
" woman of ninety.

" For some minutes we can laugh at these follies, but
" indignation and contempt soon get the better of your
" mirth, and the laugh is turned into a sneer.   I own I
" was soon tired of them; though some things are so
" strangely fancied, that it may well excuse a little
" mirth, even from the most rigid Cynic.

" The

" The family Statues are charming; they have been
" done from some old pictures, and make a most ve-
" nerable appearance. He has dressed them out from
" head to foot, in new and elegant suits of marble; and
" indeed the effect it produces is more ridiculous than
" any thing you can conceive. Their shoes are all of
" black marble, their stockings generally of red; their
" clothes are of different colours, blue, green, and va-
" riegated, with a rich lace of giall' antique. The pe-
" riwigs of the men, and head-dresses of the ladies, are
" of fine white; so are their shirt, with long flowing
" ruffles of alabaster. The walls of the house are
" covered with some fine basso-relievo's of white marble,
" in a good taste: these he could not well take out,
" or alter, so he has only added immense frames to them.
" Each frame is composed of four large marble tables.

" The author and owner of this ingenious collection is a
" poor miserable lean figure, shivering at a breeze, and
" seems to be afraid of every body he speaks to; but
" (what surprized me) I have heard him talk speciously
" enough on several occasions. He is one of the richest
" subjects in the island, and it is thought he has not laid
" out less than twenty thousand pounds in the creation
" of this world of monsters and chimeras.—He certainly
" might have fallen upon some way to prove himself a
" fool at a cheaper rate. However, it gives bread to a
" number of poor people, to whom he is an excellent
" master. His house at Palermo is a good deal in the
" same style; his carriages are covered with plates of
" brass, so that I really believe some of them are musket
" proof.

" The government has had serious thoughts of de-
" molishing the regiment of monsters he has placed
" round

" round his houfe; but as he is humane and inoffenfive,
" and as this would certainly break his heart, they have
" as yet forborne.   However, the feeing of them by
" women with child, is faid to have been already at-
" tended with very unfortunate circumftances; feveral
" living monfters having been brought forth in the
" neighbourhood.   The ladies complain, that they dare
" no longer take an airing in the Bagaria, becaufe
" fome hideous form always haunts their imagina-
" tion for fome time after: their hufbands too, it is
" faid, are as little fatisfied with the great. variety
" of horns.   *Brydone's Tour.*

(4) " The firft mufic of the Romans came from the
" Etrufcans: it was rude, and without principles; but
" they afterwards tranfported the Grecian mufic into
" Italy.   The firft Roman who wrote on mufic, was the
" famous Architect Vitruvius.   If Greece had her Ti-
" motheus and her Tyrteus, who produced fuch great
" effects on their hearers, Italy had her Stradella and
" Palma, who alfo, as it is faid, did aftonifhing things.
" Stradella, by playing on the violin, foftened the heart
" of a villain, who intended to have murdered him.
" Palma, a Neapolitan Singer, fuffered himfelf to be
" taken by a Creditor, who came to arreft him; to
" whofe menaces and injurious terms Palma only re-
" plied, by finging feveral airs, and accompanying him-
" felf on the harpfichord.   The Creditor's choler eva-
" porated, by degrees, and he was at laft fo perfectly
" calm, that he not only remitted the debt, but gave
" Palma ten pieces of gold, to affift him to pay his other
" Creditors (*a*)."

GREEK

(*a*) Brydone, in the fecond volume of his Tour, relates an
Anecdote of Farinelli: that having a pathetic Air to fing to a
Tyrant,

GREEK MUSICIANS.

" *Antimachus* was a great Muſician, and compoſed
" ſeveral Poems (*a*). One day, while reading in an
" aſſembly, he ſaw all his auditors began to be weary,
" and ſucceſſively to retire ; but Plato ſtill remaining,
" he exclaimed, *I will continue to read, for Plato alone is*
" *worth a multitude.*

" *Damophiles,* the wife of Pamphiles and friend of
" Sappho, compoſed hymns, which were ſung in honour
" of Diana. After the example of Sappho, ſhe held
" aſſemblies, where young women of ſuperior under-
" ſtanding came to learn Poetry and Muſic. Damo-
" philes compoſed ſeveral Poems.

" *Lamia*, the moſt celebrated flute-player of her time,
" was regarded as a prodigy, for her beauty, wit, and
" abilities. Plutarch and Atheneus aſſure us ſhe re-
" ceived, from all parts, the greateſt honours.

" *Nanno, Nemeade, Telezilla-Nerea,* were alſo fa-
" mous female Muſicians.

" The celebrated Thymele, invented the Theatrical
" Dance, &c."

" This catalogue is equally intereſting and extenſive in
" the work of M. de la Borde ; but I ſhall confine my-
" ſelf (having no other view than that of exciting emu-
" lation) to extract from this work a ſhort account of
" the moſt celebrated modern Female Muſicians.

Tyrant, who had taken him and his miſtreſs priſoners, the Actor,
who played the Tyrant, and who was to have refuſed his requeſt,
was ſo affected that he forgot his part, melted into tears, and
claſped his Captive in his arms.

(*a*) Poets, among the Greeks, were all Muſicians. Pindar ſet
his own Odes, and ſang them at the Olympic Games ; and it is
well known, that the famous Corinna five times bore away the
prize from Pindar.

" *Mar-*

" *Marguerita Archinta*, of a great family at Milan,
" joined to the graces of perfon, the agreeable talents
" of Poetry and Mufic. She wrote many fongs and
" madrigals, and fet them herfelf. She lived about the
" beginning of the fixteenth century.

" *Julia Vareza*, a Nun, was admired for her mufical
" ablities and excellent finging. She alfo wrote good
" Poetry.

" *Maria Marguerita Cofta*, a Roman, was a woman of
" vaft erudition, and applied herfelf, with fuccefs, to
" various branches of Literature. She wrote feveral
" poetical Operas.

" *Fauftina Bordoni*, a Venetian, and wife to the cele-
" brated compofer John-Adolphus Haffe, furnamed *il*
" *Saffone*, was a finger of the firft clafs, and invented a
" new kind of manner, which required furprizing exe-
" cution, neatnefs, and admirable precifion. She had
" the art powerfully to fuftain her voice and take her
" breath, without being perceived. She appeared at
" the Theatre of Venice, in 1716.

" *Dauphine de Sartre*, wife to the *Marquis de Robias*,
" was perfectly acquainted with ancient and modern
" Philofophy, Algebra, and other branches of the Ma-
" thematics. Mufic was her amufement ; fhe compofed
" with facility, fang well, and played on the harpfichord,
" the orbo, and lute. She died at Arles, in 1685.

" *Elizabeth Claude Jacquet de la Guerre*, born at Paris,
" gave proofs, during her earlieft infancy, of extraordi-
" nary mufical abilities. At fifteen, fhe played the
" harpfichord before the King: Madame de Montefpan
" kept her three or four years. She married Marin de
" la Guerre, an organift, and gave the world Cephalus
" and Procris (the words by Duché) three books of
" Cantatas,

" Cantatas, a Collection of Harpfichord Leffons, ano-
" ther of Sonatas, and a Te Deum for the King's re-
" covery, with grand choruffes, which was performed in
" the Chapel of the Louvre, 1721. She died in 1729.

" *Madame la Marquife de la Mézangère* was born in
" 1693, and played excellently on the harpfichord. She
" alfo underftood compofition perfectly, but would ne-
" never publifh her works. *Madame la Marquife de*
" *Gange*, her daughter, who died in 1741, played equally
" well on the harpfichord, though fhe never had any
" mafter but her mother. Madame de la Mézangère
" likewife taught a boy, who made fo great a progrefs,
" that he became teacher to the Queen and Royal Fa-
" mily of France.

" *Jean-Marie le Clair* was born at Lyons, and origi-
" nally a Dancer at Rouen. By fome odd accident, the
" famous Dupré played the violin at the fame time in
" the orcheftra of the fame Theatre; but being each
" diffatisfied with themfelves, they each did juftice to
" their talents, and changed profeffions. Dupré became
" the greateft Dancer that ever exifted, and le Clair
" opened a new career to harmony. He was murdered,
" no one knows how as he was entering his own houfe,
" after he had been fupping abroad, on the 22d of Octo-
" ber at night, 1764."—*Effai fur la Mufique.*

END OF THE FOURTH VOLUME.